CODA

Tales from a church musician

Edward Virgo

CODA

Tales from a church musician

E. Virgo 2023

Edward Virgo

Copyright © 2023 Edward Virgo

All rights reserved

ISBN 9798391773764

Dedication

Shelagh

Catherine

Kaylem

and

Dorothy (1920 – 1985)

Contents

842 842 1

A death in C minor 8

A mitred head conceals 13

Amanuensis 19

An eye and ear deceived? 24

A most peculiar doubling 26

A Period Faithful And Holy 31

A wilful harmonium 36

Boy with a tin whistle 40

Cancelled 44

Cindy and Burney 50

Console gremlins 56

Diabolus in musica 60

Hillfire 65

Jerry Molto's magic one-man band 72

Lady Sarah's spinet 76

Liam's imaginary friend 82

Losing Laura 86

Musica de profundis 92

Santa's organ sleigh 97

Terry's church in miniature 101
The busker 105
The cats' quartet.. 109
The harmonious poltergeist 112
The harpist of Tŷ Pen Rhiw.. 117
The music box.. 125
The old organ shoes 129

842 842

It's hard to believe that such places still exist. Villages looking as if they had been fixed in time somewhere around 1950. Well, Nether Furleigh is one of those. The only concession to modernity is the satellite dishes on the two newest properties – fancy constructions designed by avant-garde architects for city types with money to burn. Life in the village is pretty quiet, apart from the sound of 4-by-4s owned by the plutocrats. (How do they manage to have wellingtons completely untainted by mud or manure?)

John and Sandra Bennett had lived in the village for more than 10 years. John was a solicitor in Upper Furleigh. Sandra was a teacher at the local college. On the surface, they seemed a quiet but sociable couple. But behind the veil, as they say, all was not well. Rumours had been circulating for some time that one or other of them had been having an affair, and there was a lot of whispering and net curtain twitching going on. On occasion, arguments could be heard, but local busy-bodies avid for violence were disappointed. However, they were to have cause for greater excitement than they could have anticipated.

On a Sunday morning in May last year, a neighbour had noticed that the front door of the Bennetts' house was half open, and thought she would indulge her curiosity. She probably wished she hadn't. She called out but there was no answer. Now you or I probably wouldn't have the cheek to go uninvited up the stairs in someone else's house, even if the door was open. However, she went up to the main bedroom at the top of the stairs, perhaps hoping for a Peeping Tom thrill, catching the Bennetts 'at it' under the duvet. What actually greeted her was the sight of Sandra Bennett sprawled on the bed, but very much not alive.

The police came, and the pathologist was quickly on the scene. Not much sign of a struggle. An overturned stool, a discarded slipper, and a small bag whose contents had been emptied on the floor. Sandra Bennett had been strangled, and so violently that the rope or cord used had cut into her neck, drawing blood.

The gossip was rife with speculation. Had John Bennett 'lost it'? Was there a love-triangle leading to the tragedy? With a small community, the task of interviewing everyone might be expected to be straightforward. But John Bennett was nowhere to be found. There was someone else missing: Jane Croft. She was also a teacher at the school (husband Samuel ran a bookshop in Walmsley). Samuel said Jane had gone to visit her mother up North for a couple of days. He said that he had been at home since Friday, but his alibi was insecure because there were no witnesses to confirm it. Someone else without an alibi was David Hurford the church organist. He lived alone, but had been linked with Sandra Bennett by the rumour-mongers in the village. With the above exceptions, everyone was interviewed by Inspector Charles Moran and Detective Sergeant Ian Dymcock. Neither was very popular in the local force, acquiring the 'combo' title 'Moron and Dimprick'.

Bennett eventually reappeared. He claimed he'd been up in London for a meeting and had stayed over – hence his absence. The police were able to corroborate his story about the London meeting, but there was no witness evidence covering the rest of the time. He could, perhaps, have come home, killed his wife, and driven back to London to sustain his story.

But attention shifted to Hurford. After all, if Bennett was elsewhere, he couldn't have killed Sandra. Hurford was around during the entire period. But there was something else. Some people using the Stanford Arms pub were in the habit of leaving their cars there overnight and either walking home or taking a taxi. Hurford's car was seen at the pub, but he explained that he wasn't at the pub that night, but that his car had been left there the previous night because its battery was flat. He was waiting for someone from the garage to get it going or maybe borrow some jump leads.

However, in a separate development, someone at the taxi firm, Cooke's Cars, said that they had received a call for a cab to pick up two people from the pub to take them to 12, Ash Lane – the Bennett house. The caller had made the call in the name of Bennett.

Moran and Dymcock interviewed Hurford again and obtained a warrant to search his house. On the night in question he had claimed that he was practising in the church, late, between 10 and 11 p.m. but there were no witnesses for this. The Rev. Tom Attwood had seen a light on in the church at about 11.00, but on entering the church found it empty. The lights in the organ loft had been left on, possibly in error. Attwood had been going to mention it the next day.

The police searched Hurford's house. Dymcock opened Hurford's music case. Nothing of interest. An anthology of 18th century organ voluntaries and a Novello volume of Bach preludes and fugues. As he replaced them in the bag, a piece of paper fell out. He thought he'd pocket it, just in case. Hurford was interviewed again, this time with a lawyer present.

'You say you weren't at the Stanford Arms on that Saturday evening.' Moran began. 'You deny having an affair with the deceased, or booking a taxi to take you both to Ash Lane, is that correct?'

Hurford, irritated, replied,' My lawyer here might advise me to say 'No Comment', but this whole thing is ridiculous. There might have been some malicious rumours about me and Sandra, but an affair? Rubbish! Yes, we shared an interest in music, but so do I and Tom Attwood, but you're not suggesting I'm having a relationship with him.'

'Then', said Moran portentously, puffing himself up as if about to deliver a killer blow, 'perhaps you would care to explain this.'

He slid a plastic pocket across the table. It contained a piece of A5 paper. On one side there were some numbers – straightforward – they were the phone numbers of the local dentist and the pharmacy.

'No! The other side,' Moran gesticulated.

Hurford turned the paper over. On that side in a bit of a scrawl, it read:

        Bennett
   8 4 2 8 4 2 (couple)
        10, 20

'This was found in your music bag, Mr. Hurford. On that night, someone claiming to be Bennett ordered a taxi from Cooke's Cars for 10.20 p.m. That is the phone number for Cooke's Cars, as you probably know. Would you like to explain how you come to have this paper with this number on and the name 'Bennett', stipulating a couple and a time 10.20, which is exactly the time requested in the phone call? Are you denying you are the person who ordered that cab, for you and Sandra Bennett? You went home with her, didn't you – you rowed, lost your temper and strangled her, didn't you?'

Hurford replied indignantly 'Absolutely not!'

They didn't really have enough to hold him, but Moran still thought he had his man.

Hurford told Attwood about the whole business. Attwood was shocked, but was curious about the lights being left on in the church.

'Sorry, Tom, I must have forgotten. Fit of absent-mindedness.'

'The trouble, David, is that if I mention this to the police, they'll say you deliberately left the lights on to create the alibi that you were practising in the church at the time of the murder.'

Hurford took the point, but went on.

'Then there's the business with the piece of paper they found in my music bag. I'd never seen it before, but they think it incriminates me.'

Attwood was curious. Although the police now had the paper, Hurford could remember what was written on it. After hearing the details, Attwood paused.

'Where did you say it was found?'

Hurford replied, 'In my music bag.'

'Then, I think I need to have a word with our inspector', Attwood said.

Attwood asked to see Moran. The next day, he attended the police station.

'Well, what do you want to see me about?', Moran began bluntly.

'David Hurford says you have a piece of paper whose contents you put before him in interview?'

'What concern of that is yours?'

'Forgive me', Attwood retorted, 'if I find your attitude offensive. If you want upright citizens to assist you, may I recommend you attend a different charm school?'

Moran winced, and Dymcock tried to suppress a snigger.

'If I might be permitted to continue', Attwood said, 'the piece of paper is not his but mine. Mr Hurford and I share an interest in organ music. I'm just an amateur, but now and again I borrow some of his music and practice when I can. Not long ago, I borrowed an anthology of pieces. One piece I was working on was a voluntary by John Bennett – something of a co-incidence, I know, but this John Bennett lived in the 18th century. The numbers on the paper are not a phone number, but a scheme of registration for playing the piece. Had I been more careful, I might have made it clear that 8, 4 and 2 indicate the stops to be used on the two manuals. 'Couple' means the coupling together of the keyboards. By the way, the numbers 10 and 20 are bar numbers. You mistook a comma for a period.'

Moran was numbed by the technicalities at this point. Attwood was close to laughter.

'And I thought it was us religious types that made mountains out of coincidences. Since I don't want to waste any more of your valuable time, I shall bid you farewell. But I think Mr. Hurford might appreciate a cloud being lifted from his head.'

Attwood left with a spring in his step.

'That cunt gets right up my fucking nose, Dymcock', Moran muttered, confirming his Neanderthal credentials.

The police went back to the Stanford Arms and had a word with the landlord, John Burley. He confirmed that Hurford had not been in the pub on that night. But Sandra Bennett had been, as was already known. She wasn't with Hurford – she was with Samuel Croft. About 10 p.m., she had gone outside. Croft had followed her shortly afterwards. Burley thought he heard a car drive off a few minutes later.

After this, things took a rapid new direction. Croft was interviewed, his home searched, and a piece of rough twine with Sandra Bennett's blood on it was found in a tool box in his garage. The absence of Jane Croft and John Bennett was explained by the fact that they were having an affair and had had their own tryst in a flat in London. Her mother had confirmed that she had not been to see her that weekend. Hurford was relieved at last – but paused to think how close he came to being ruined by a piece of paper.

A death in C minor

Claybourne United Reformed Church is a Gothic Revival building in red sandstone. The minister, Lucinda Latham, had been in post for five years. During that time, Claybourne had been experiencing what many churches were experiencing – a decline in membership. A building that once hosted congregations of several hundred now echoed to a modest gathering of 60. There had been the inevitable tensions of one kind or another. Both church and elders' meetings were frequently bad-tempered affairs, the more heated in direct proportion to the triviality of the points raised.

Among the tensions that persisted were those between the organist Arthur Hayes and certain members of the congregation. A few years before, he had had succeeded the late Brian Cooke who had been in post for 40 years until his death at the age of 86. Some people could not really accept Arthur Hayes, partly because he wasn't Brian Cooke, and partly because he had tried to raise the calibre of church music. There were always people who presumed to pontificate on matters theological and musical while being massively ignorant about both. One such person was Trevor Burke. ('impolitely described by one member as 'Burke in name and in nature, too') On one occasion, after Hayes had completed a performance of a powerful Bach prelude and fugue as a recessional, he was accosted by Burke as he was descending from the organ loft.

'Do you have to play so loud? I didn't like that piece at all. Why can't you play something decent? Why can't you play something by Bach?'

Hayes replied 'What did you think that was?'

Burke stalked off, muttering under his breath. Sadly, however, the 'grumblers' mafia' were to get their revenge, owing to a serious error of judgement by Hayes himself.

Hayes' enthusiasm had got the better of him. He was given to tampering with the instrument, and eventually arranged with the organ builders, Cross and Bowker, to add further stops to the Great. All this was done without consulting minister, elders or church meeting. The resulting work cost a considerable sum of money, and the first anyone knew about it was when the Treasurer received the invoice.

Lucinda visited Hayes at home where he lived alone. She told him that he had completely exceeded his remit as musical director, and his employment was terminated forthwith. This amounted more to a reputational humiliation than a financial blow, since he was a teacher at the local school. However, the result was that the organ fell silent. A church member, Margaret Withey, a rather nervous elderly spinster, undertook to play the piano on Sundays. No effort was made to replace Hayes.

But Hayes' troubles were far from over. A few weeks after the church 'debacle', complaints about Hayes were made by two sets of parents, alleging that he had molested their young sons – pupils in the Primary division of the school. He was interviewed by the police, having been temporarily suspended on full pay. Despite the fact that there was as yet no solid evidence to support the accusations, the rumour mill was rolling and Hayes became the target of abuse. Trevor Burke delighted in leading the charge, confronting Hayes in the street,

'So, you're not only a spendthrift nearly bankrupting our church, you're also a bloody pervert. You should get out of here and not come back. They should put you away for years!'

The 'Burke brigade' had got more than they had wished for. Margaret Withey was compliant, not venturing beyond hymn standards played at Mogodon tempo. Meanwhile, the parents and their allegedly abused boys were also interviewed by the police. They had intended to interview Hayes, but he had quite suddenly disappeared. There had now been no sign of him for several weeks. There had been unlikely sightings – one on a Cross-Channel ferry, another on a train to Bristol, but nothing of real substance.

Lucinda Latham thought that despite everything, the organ should be examined and assessed. By now, it would be badly out of tune, and recent bad weather would have accelerated its deterioration. Perhaps its replacement with a modern digital instrument might be considered.

Ray Goodwin and Colin Best had worked together for two decades, and had regularly maintained the instrument. They told Lucinda that it was likely that there could be further considerable expense incurred in trying to make the instrument playable, let alone undertaking major overhaul.

'If the leathers have gone, or some of the wooden components have split or broken, there could be a host of problems. But we'll have a look at it for you.', said Ray Goodwin.

Access to the organ chamber was by a side door to the right of the console. It was left unlocked as a general rule, so Ray and Colin went upstairs and turned the knob on the door. They couldn't open it.

'That's odd', Ray said.

While they were standing there, they felt a chill in the air, and there was a strange smell.

'It's like a stale fart', Colin observed.

They called down to Lucinda just as she was about to leave, and explained the problem. There was a spare key in the downstairs office. As they were going up the stairs, Ray stopped half-way.

'Hang on. If no-one's been up here and locked the door, then it must have been locked from the inside.'

They unlocked the door and entered the organ chamber. They were not prepared for what they saw. There, hanging from a cross beam between the swell box and the main casing was the body of Arthur Hayes. He must have been hanging there for weeks. The key to the door was found in his pocket, along with a note expressing despair and regret, but emphatically no admission of guilt regarding the children. In fact, it subsequently emerged that the boys had made the whole thing up. It was a cheap piece of malicious behaviour with terrible consequences.

It was now Trevor Burke's turn to suffer the odium of others. One church member approached him and called him 'an obnoxious old shit'. Suffice to say he was thereafter conspicuous by his absence from the church and its meetings.

Lucinda longed for the day when all this tragic affair was over and some normality restored. She longed to hear the organ again, having shared Arthur Hayes' enthusiasm for it. She did not have long to wait.

One evening, she had gone into the church to collect some flyers from the vestry. It was then that she heard the sound of the organ. Who on earth could be up there? She stepped into the chancel. She could see the organ light was on. She nervously went up the stairs, and stood, looking with amazement at the console. The instrument was still playing – keys and pedals moving as if being played by invisible hands and feet. She recognised the piece: Bach's Prelude and Fugue in C minor, BWV537, a piece with a rather tragic atmosphere, which she had heard Arthur Hayes play at funerals and Remembrance services. After 8 minutes the piece ended, the light went out, the organ fell silent. Lucinda stumbled around feeling for the switch of the stair light.

Had Arthur Hayes had the last word?

A mitred head conceals

Marcus Berg was eccentric. In some ways, he conformed to an old-fashioned stereotype of an elderly, absent-minded academic. For all that, he had been something of an expert on mediaeval history and archaeology, being the author of several books and numerous articles, some relating to substantial finds, of buried coins, brooches and some military items as well. Among his major obsessions was a search for a legendary gold cross associated with Kirkston Abbey, just a few miles from the university.

The story goes that in the 15th century, a gold cross had been made and hidden in some special location by the monks. The Abbey had miraculously survived the Dissolution, so it was assumed that the cross was still safe. The last hint of its existence was in an old manuscript from around 1600, where something answering to its description was listed in an inventory of the abbey's treasures. One element of the original legend was the claim that, if the cross ever left the abbey or was stolen or melted down for gain, the abbey itself would be destroyed.

Berg worked on this project for many years, and carried it on after he retired. He was not alone with this obsession. It was rumoured in the department that he belonged to a secret group pursuing the search. The group even had a title – 'The Crucians'. It was estimated that there were about six people in this group, including, it was alleged, a high court judge, a vice=chancellor of another university, and a major industrialist. At one time, there was speculation that the group was in fact a paedophile ring, but there was in fact no substance to this scurrilous suggestion. No-one in the department took it seriously.

Berg had been retired 12 years when he died. He never married, and it fell to his sister and his nephew and niece to try and clear his property. His study presented them with a major task. His bookshelves were a librarian's nightmare, and his large mahogany desk resembled a land-fill site. His relatives approached the department for assistance, assuming that there might be material of some interest to be salvaged from the mountain Berg had accumulated over several decades. Some of us took up the offer and his relatives seemed happy to leave us to get on with it. We spent several days at the property.

Before he died, Berg had started to dispose of some material himself. At the end of the rear garden there was a large old oil drum that he had been using to burn rubbish. It was packed with ashes and some incompletely burned manuscripts. We guessed that he might have been destroying 'sensitive' material relating to the Crucians. At all events, we had found nothing of such significance in the study, until I decided to tackle the drawers in his desk. Nothing particularly interesting to begin with – old diaries, notepads, bulldog clips. I shook out the diaries as I discarded them in the wastepaper basket. As I shook the last one, a folded piece of A4 paper fell out on the desk. I opened it and spread it out on the leather desk-top. There was an array of numbers followed by what looked like a rather cryptic instruction:

48 3 60 15 54
18 27 36 27 63 57
57 48   27 54 27 60 63 57
'Beneath these in repose a mitred head conceals'

We all looked puzzled, wondering what this could mean. Was this a surviving coded communication between Berg and his Crucian friends? Naturally, the word 'conceals' fuelled our curiosity. Was this piece of paper like a map reference locating buried treasure, redolent of stories about pirates and exotic desert islands?

The numbers seemed odd for co-ordinates – West, East …? And each number sequence was longer than the one above. Perhaps they indicated the number of paces in a given direction, say '48 paces, then turn left 3 paces, then 15 and finally 54' to…. where exactly? And if these were distances, were they for inside or outside locations?

This was not going to be easy. We decided to finish up. We told Berg's relatives that we had exhausted our searches and retrieved what we could. It was left to them to dispose of the rest of the contents of the study. They were hardly excited by the prospect, but were grateful for our assistance. We had at least gone some way towards tidying up the room and reduced the risk of unstable piles of books and journals toppling on people's heads!

I thought of asking a colleague from the Mathematics department to have a look at this set of figures. We sat with our cups of coffee, staring at the numbers.

'There's one thing you can say right away', he said. 'All these figures are threes or multiples of three.

For instance, the first one, 48, is 3 x 16. 60 is obviously 3 x 20, and so on.'

Eventually, he wrote out all the original figures that had been trebled, giving the following result:

```
      16  1 20  5 18
       6  9 12  9 21 19
   19 16  9 18  9 20 21 19
```

'Well, where does that get us?' I asked. 'Looks like we've exchanged one set of figures for another.' I was still puzzled.

'Well, I don't think we can reduce these further. There's some repetition which suggests to me that we've got alphabetical substitution. I mean, these numbers stand for letters. Take the first one: 16 is the number of the 16th letter of the alphabet which is 'P'. let's try this out on the rest.'

We were both amazed at the outcome:

PATER

FILIUS

SPIRITUS

'So now you have to find these somewhere with a mitred head below. 'mitred head' – sounds like a bishop, doesn't it? I wish you luck with that one!'

Several of us from the department got together the following day and decided to go to the Abbey, armed with our new information. The task – to find a mitred head beneath the three persons of the Trinity. We surmised that we would be looking for the tomb of a bishop below an inscription of some sort. As there were four of us we split into two pairs searching opposite sides of the nave. There were also side chapels to investigate. After an hour of slow, careful search, we found the tomb of a bishop Martin de Lacey. Sure enough, there he was reclining in effigy, and on a small arch immediately above were the three words my mathematical colleague had de-coded.

'What now?' we asked.

Then we looked more closely at the bishop's head. It was 'resting' on a stone cushion. One of us suggested we try and see if the cushion was moveable. Two of us leaned over and applied some pressure to it and contrary to our expectations it started to move. After further effort, we were able to slide it out from under the bishop's head which now remained unsupported, which looked very odd. The removal of the stone cushion now revealed a cavity below the bishop's head. Fortunately, I had brought a small torch. Shining this directly into the void, we could now see a small cloth bundle. It took a little time to manoeuvre the item out of the very confined space.

We took it to a table in the side aisle and opened the bundle. We gasped as we found ourselves looking at a beautiful gold cross approximately 30 centimetres in height, encrusted with jewels of various colours. This was what Berg and his friends had been protecting.

We were obliged to approach the church authorities for permission to remove the cross so that it could be taken to the local museum for examination and dating. After a fortnight, permission was granted and the cross taken away. The intention was that it would be returned to the Abbey and an appropriate and secure place found where it could be publicly displayed.

Halfway through this period, there was a violent storm one evening and lightning struck the Abbey roof, which caught fire. Fortunately, the fire brigade managed to extinguish it before much damage was caused. Some people started to mutter that the fire was a consequence of the removal of the cross from the building. Such is superstition.

In due course the cross was returned to the Abbey. We attended a sort of ceremony where it was installed in a specially made case with thick protective glass, in a niche prepared not far from the de Lacey tomb. The Crucians may not have approved, but at least the cross was available for others to see. As a nice touch the abbey organist Michael Camidge played Bach's Prelude and Fugue in E Flat. After all, this had been a story of 'threeness'.

Amanuensis

Professor Leonard Copthorne had for some years been Head of Department at the University of Lanchester. He was a renowned specialist on music of the baroque era, and especially keyboard music for harpsichord and organ. Over the years, he had become involved in some of the familiar academic disputes over authorship and attribution. Among these were those relating to J. S. Bach. For long enough there had been arguments over the authorship of the Eight Short Preludes and Fugues BWV553 – 60. Some were confident that they were not Bach's work but written by his pupil Johann Krebs, or perhaps even his father Tobias.

Leonard Copthorne was himself sceptical, although he entertained the possibility that they could be immature works by Krebs when he was experimenting with different ideas. Immature, because the material was relatively briefly developed, and there were, for instance, none of the extended pedal passages typical of Krebs' confirmed works. So it was that Copthorne came to have a special interest in Krebs. His researches took him abroad to Germany, to Zwickau where Krebs had held a lowly position. But ironically, it was to be nearer home that Copthorne was to have his most unusual experience.

Lanchester Oldgate Street has few shops left other than estate agents, restaurants, and smaller branches of two major supermarket chains. Up a side street there are one or two antique shops (some would say 'junk shops') and a curious premises vending 'adult' toys. Copthorne would sometimes linger by the window of the latter, more out of amazement than arousal, before proceeding to the labyrinths of dusty remnants further up the street. The first of these, Sillcotts, dealt with a range of items, including musical ones, although there were mountains of what many would describe as 'Victorian crud'. Just occasionally, Copthorne had managed to disinter some more worthy specimens, like bound volumes (landscape format) of organ works by various composers from Mendelssohn to Vierne. But he had not found anything of interest there for some time. Not that the owner was bothered. He seemed like some throwback – trapped in a 120-year time warp somewhere around the 1890's.

Malephants, two doors up, was no less untidy, but run by an enthusiastic young entrepreneur, only too eager to assist. However, Copthorne was happy to potter and rummage about on his own. It was while engaged in one of these 'excavations', that he made an interesting find. At the bottom of a pile of otherwise unexceptional material was a large leather-bound volume with a title in gold lettering on the cover. 'Praeludien und Fugen Band 1'. Inside, was the fuller title identifying the composer as one Johann Ludwig Krebs, and a publisher, J. U. Haffner, Nurnberg, 1744.

Copthorne was excited by this find and haggled over the price with the young shop owner. He felt satisfied to have purchased it for just £85. Perhaps if the young man had been more steeped in matters musical, the outlay might have been considerably greater. But

Copthorne was a regular customer, and transactions were usually cordial.

Once home, Copthorne looked through the volume, which was in splendid condition considering its age. He was a little mystified how it had turned up in the shop in Lanchester. At some point, it must have been brought over from Germany, but when and by whom was destined to remain a mystery. As far as he could see, all the pieces were familiar and had subsequently appeared in more modern editions (Peters, Breitkopf, etc.).

One curious feature of the volume was that at the back, there were several pages with blank staves – fifteen in fact. Copthorne was briefly reminded of all the lacunae in Bach's original manuscript of the Orgelbuchlein, but it seemed a little odd for what seemed to be an otherwise complete publisher's edition lying on the desk in front of him. He now had to consider what to do with the volume. He felt it should be valued and ideally lodged in the university or departmental library. He would not want to see it auctioned and disappear into some selfish private owner's collection Such things should be in principle available more widely.

Whether his excitement had got the better of him or his cheese on toast in the late evening had threatened his sleep, he had a very strange dream. He seemed to be seated at his desk with the music volume in front of him, open at the first of the blank pages. He then found himself writing on the staves as if his hands were being controlled by some invisible agent. Gradually the staves filled up with notes and he soon began to realise that he was seeing another prelude unfolding before his eyes. After a few pages, this section, with a substantial pedal part, was completed. Then he found himself penning a fugue. After what seemed an age, his hand came to a halt with the final cadence. Sifting through the pages, he now saw that he had written (or been made to write) an entire prelude and fugue in the key of E Flat, and one he had never seen before in any of Kreb's published works.

The dream ended abruptly at that point and although he tossed and turned a little thereafter, nothing else occurred before he woke at eight in the morning. He wandered down the stairs, feeling slightly dazed. After breakfast, he went into his study and saw the music volume lying open where he had left it the previous night. He stared at it with incredulity. Despite what he had dreamt, those last fifteen pages were blank as before. Yes, it had all been a dream, albeit very vivid. But in spite of that he wanted to recall the piece he had 'produced' in that dream – it seemed so in keeping with the other material printed. Although an experienced player, it was a big ask to recall such a piece on the strength of one 'reading' (or writing). Perhaps a second coffee might enhance the memory.

Copthorne turned the empty pages. Was he hoping for inspiration staring at the blank staves? Then he looked at the back cover. There seemed to be a long slit in the lining and something poking out of it. His fingers couldn't get a grip, so he went off and found a pair of tweezers in a cupboard drawer. He gradually and gently teased out a thick wad of paper. Fifteen sheets of manuscript paper filled with music – the music he had dreamed he had written down during the night. But this music was printed. It was almost as if it had got lost or been omitted from the collection in the rest of the volume. He decided he must attempt to play it – but rather than subject the actual manuscript to risk, he photocopied it and took the copy with him to the large music room in the department. This room housed a large three manual digital instruments used for both concerts and student examinations and allowed for period registrations as required. He booked a slot for the following day when no-one else would be practising.

He had thought himself lucky with his purchase, but this was a bonus. He knew that a process of authentication lay ahead, there would be eyebrows raised at his account of the discovery, but for the moment he could at least enjoy playing the piece. It lasted about 12 minutes, allowing for some slips and unintended dissonances, but he felt reasonably satisfied.

He was just relaxing, and in a contemplative mood, when he felt a hand on his shoulder. He turned round and was quite startled to find a man, middle-aged and in 18th century clothing, standing by him. The man smiled kindly and said "Ich bin dankbar. Ich segne dich!" and promptly vanished.

An eye and ear deceived?

The van der Vaart violin is a famous attraction at Chatsworth. This day, I saw a visiting party crowded around the door looking with amazement at this feat of trompe l'oeil painting. One person reached out to touch the door, incredulous. Others laughed while concealing not a little embarrassment at themselves being almost taken in by the trick. The group moved on, and I was left alone, contemplating this small wonder, which was created in about 1723. One could readily imagine an instrument of this type being used to play music from the baroque era. But what happened next, be it imagination, reverie, or hallucination, I leave you to decide.

One of the guides remained in the room, eyeing me closely. He obviously did not share the experience I had as I lingered by that door. I don't know whether he had a suspicion that I might be a potential thief with my eye on the porcelain pieces on display in the cabinet nearby, but it quickly became apparent to him that I had become fixated on this item of artistic trickery.

As I stood there, it was as if an invisible hand had reached out and lifted the instrument off the iron hook on the door. Then it seemed that a second hand took the bow and its invisible owner started to play a whole suite of pieces – gigues, sarabandes, gavottes, and the like. Some brought composers like Handel and Bach to mind. Some other pieces were like folk dances. The guide must have thought me very odd, swinging about in time to the music, to which he seemed to be deaf. The player continued for several more minutes, after which the violin seemed to be suspended in the air and it looked as if the player was tuning the instrument in preparation for further performance.

'Can I help you, sir?' the guide asked, wondering why I had stayed so long in the room, fixated on the door. 'You are rather 'hooked' on that illusion. Don't miss out on some of the other interesting things here. I don't want to lock you in when we close at 5.00 p.m.'

The guide gave a mischievous smile. If he only knew what I had experienced. But there was more to come. After ten more minutes playing, things went silent again. Then, quite suddenly, as if through a mist, a figure appeared in period costume, smiled and bowed, returned the violin to the iron peg on the door and vanished from sight.

A most peculiar doubling

Martin Alcock arrived at St. Luke's just before 10.00 a.m. He was greeted by Anne Lockhart in the porch. He had a conversation with the new vicar, Rev. Wendy Cresswell. They checked some of the details of the service and then he put up the hymn numbers on the two boards on the front pillars on each side of the rood screen. A number of the congregation were already seated. Some of them were in the habit of coming early to listen to Martin play his pre-service music. There were a few others who came at the last minute, the tone deaf clique with the tin ears. These also tended to be the ones given to making ill-informed comments about everything, including the music. Others just came to gossip. For them, Martin's efforts were merely background sound to cover their idle chit-chat.

      The service commenced with the hymn 'Love Divine' sung to 'Blaenwern'. (One Welsh member preferred 'Hyfrydol', but she could hardly object to one Welsh tune rather than another.) Wendy gave her sermon on the theme of putting one's talents at the disposal of others when and wherever possible. This was a communion Sunday, so the service was longer than usual and there were more people present. Martin improvised on 'Allein Gott' as communion was served. Two quite elderly ladies (sisters) always sat at the back and then complained that they couldn't hear anything. They themselves, however, were highly audible, with that sort of loud whisper that would have been the envy of any stage prompt at the town theatre.

After the service, Martin joined those who stayed behind for coffee and biscuits. Some of them, at least, thanked him for his recessional piece, the Maestoso first movement of Rheinberger's 13th Organ Sonata. Mission accomplished, thought Martin. And so it was, in a manner of speaking…. except…

Martin Alcock arrived at St. Mary's just before 10.00. He was greeted by Frank Wright, the verger. He then had a brief word with Ron Davidson, the Rector. Frank Wright offered to put up the hymn numbers. Martin made his way up the stairs to the organ loft. (Two spiral flights like something in a mediaeval turret, and just as badly lit.) There was a reasonable turn-out on this particular morning, so there was a prospect of a congregation in good voice.

The service commenced with 'Let us with a gladsome mind' sung to 'Monkland'. No communion at St. Mary's this week. Probably just as well. Ron tended to ramble on a bit. Some good ideas, but flying in rather loose formation, you might say. Old George Herbert, who, being of some girth, filled a two-person space in the back pew, was given to nodding off from time to time. Ron's sermons seemed to afford him the opportunity to catch up with his sleep, but his snoring was ever so slightly embarrassing. On this occasion, however, he caused relatively little disturbance, although he did need a prod to tell him that the service was over.

The folk at St. Mary's were not exactly sociable, and their attitude to Martin was close to being one of condescension, as if he were their servant. Of all of them, Frank Wright was the most affable and welcoming. So, he gathered up his music and left. Some people in the lobby offered a perfunctory 'good-bye' as he passed them.

It was when he woke up in hospital that Martin found himself in a state of confusion. Had he dreamt of being at the same time in two churches more than a mile apart? Yet everything was so vivid. After a few days, he began to feel less mentally 'foggy'. Then the physician came into the ward on his rounds, accompanied by two juniors.

'And how are you today, Mr. Alcock?', he began.

Martin managed to mumble a reply, but felt awkward about sounding so inarticulate.

'Well, we'll have to keep you in for observation for a bit longer. We'll try and get you up and walking about soon. Meanwhile, we'll have to do some more tests. I'll discuss things with you a bit more after those are completed. By the way, you have two visitors downstairs in reception. I said it was all right for to see you for a short while, but that you must not get tired. Martin was going to ask who the visitors were, but the staff nurse said they were on their way up – a man and a woman.

'Hello there, Martin!', said Frank approaching the bed. Behind him came Anne Lockhart.

'We were quite shocked to learn that you were in hospital. You seemed to be all right on Sunday.' Anne said.

Frank looked at her with raised eyebrows, as if to say 'What the hell is she talking about?' He turned to her and said,

'Sunday? Which Sunday? Martin was with us last Sunday!'

Anne looked quite taken aback at this.

'Oh no, Frank, he was definitely with us – I remember greeting him in the porch. That's right, isn't, Martin?'

Martin was at a loss to know how to respond. If he were to say they were both right, they would assume he was confused for medical reasons. He was starting to feel decidedly queasy and distressed. Both Anne and Frank were correct, but then surely they couldn't be, could they?

But Anne and Frank dug their heels in and refused to concede any ground. They became argumentative. The last thing Martin felt able to cope with was a verbal battle conducted across his bed. They had started to raise their voices, and other patients and their visitors began to give them hostile looks. The physician was still on the ward, and a nurse was having what looked like an urgent exchange with him, pointing in the direction of Martin's bed. He came over.

'Is there a problem?', he asked, politely urging them to be a little quieter.

Anne responded with irritation.

'Well, it's like this, doctor. Frank here swears blind that Martin was in his church last Sunday, when I know very well he was with us at that time!'

The doctor looked at the pair of them.

'What on earth are these people on about?' he thought to himself. 'Could I ask which Sunday we're talking about?' he began.

'Last Sunday', they replied in chorus.

The doctor eyed them a little sternly.

'I fear you must both be mistaken. Mr. Alcock was admitted to this hospital on the Friday before that Sunday, having suffered a seizure and a loss of consciousness. There is no way he could have been in either of your churches on that Sunday morning.'

A Period Faithful And Holy

'Better get down there and see what's going on, Jeff. Lord knows what that lot have been up to. What possessed the family to hire those bloody cowboys?'

Alan and Jeff Bateson were brothers running the town's major firm of auctioneers. They had recently got wind of a house clearance in the Stockfield Road. A rather eccentric bachelor had not long died and his relatives had decided to empty the property as quickly as possible. It had been something of a tip by all accounts, since the deceased had been a rather unsystematic collector of all manner of items, some of which were suspected of being quite valuable, others worthless tat. There was some fine porcelain, one or two Georgian silver jugs and dishes. Some of these had already found their way to Bateson's, but the brothers suspected that there might be more to be found. They didn't trust the 'cowboys', Johnson and Blake, who, lacking any real expertise, were as likely to discard something really good in the skip that had been hired and which was now rapidly filling up outside No. 45 Stockfield Road. On the other hand, they were not above pocketing small items to sell on for personal gain. (Blake had served time for fraud some years ago.)

Jeff and Alan arrived at the house in time to see two of Johnson and Blake's minions heaving a suite of broken and threadbare furniture into the skip. As they stood there, the men emerged with a large rectangular object which looked like an enormous pasting table, made of dark wood, possibly mahogany or teak. It was obviously quite heavy, given the grunting and snorting that accompanied their efforts to toss it unceremoniously into the skip.

'Wait a minute, you two!', Jeff said in a sharp tone of voice.

'Do you bother to look at what you're throwing out, you pillocks!' (Jeff was nothing if not direct.)

Despite their swearing back at him under their breath, they heaved the object back out onto the pavement and leant it against the front garden wall. Alan phoned the office and got one of his colleagues to come out with one of the larger vans. Jeff produced a tape measure. This curious object measured three by one and a half metres. It had a narrow seam all the way around, which suggested that it in fact consisted of two pieces of the same proportions. But there seemed to be no obvious way to open or separate the parts. They needed to get it back to the storeroom for closer examination.

They managed to lay this sizeable item on some trestles in the storeroom. They looked at it closely. When they were at the house, they hadn't noticed two things. On one side, there was a sequence of words carved into the wood. It was a phrase which looked as if it might have been a quotation. It read 'A Period Faithful and Holy'. What might it mean? Jeff and Alan were puzzled. Also, they found that along one of the shorter edges was a sequence of what looked initially like four knots in the wood. But they were too uniform – the same size and circular in shape.

'They look like they might be buttons, Alan', said Jeff.

At which point, Alan pressed the first button. The number 1 appeared, and with repeated pressings, the whole sequence from 1 to 10 appeared. Alan tried the other buttons, with the same result.

'Know what I think, Jeff? I think we've got something like a coded lock on this thing, but we don't know the numbers of the code. But we don't want to smash our way into this, because we might damage what's inside.'

Some years ago, the brothers had come into the possession of a coded diary belonging to an SS officer. This had been found among the effects of a retired army captain who had acquired it at the end of World War II. On that occasion, they thought it would be useful if the contents could be decoded. It would assist the process were the item to come to auction. There was always a market for militaria and suchlike – whether institutions or enthusiastic individual collectors. Alan and Jeff had an advantage here. Though they didn't advertise the fact for obvious reasons, they had a cousin Mark Cowling who worked at GCHQ in Cheltenham. He had helped out over the SS diary, and they thought they might get him to have a look at the inscription.

They invited him over for the weekend and indulged in their passion for fishing. On the Saturday, they went to the auction rooms and gave Mark an opportunity to look at the inscription.

The first thing that struck him was the fact that all the words began with upper-case letters, including the word 'And'. Perhaps there was some significance in this capitalisation.

'One obvious thing to try in these cases is the idea of letters substituting for numbers or possibly other letters.', Mark began. He took a piece of paper.

'Let's go straight for the numbers/letters substitution'. This would give us the sequence

$$A = 1, P = 16, F = 6, A = 1 \text{ and } H = 8$$
$$\text{So } 1,16,1,8$$

But then there was an immediate snag. The buttons at the end of the object didn't go beyond 10. Mark paused.

'Let's think about this for a moment. Presumably this inscription has something to do with what's inside. A 'period' suggests a length of time – in which whatever it is that is faithful and holy is present.'

Then Mark paused again.

'Hang on! What else does the word 'period' suggest to you?'

The brothers looked at each other. Jeff snorted with laughter.

'Sorry, I'm being indelicate. I was thinking about Carol. She's going through that 'time of the month' as they call it. Not funny. But it kind of popped into my mind.'

Mark nodded.

'Yes, I understand that, but there's something a bit more obvious than that. 'Period' is another word for a full stop. Now we would end up with

$$1.1618$$

'But where is there a way of getting beyond '10' with the buttons, asked Jeff. 'Perhaps you should have pressed again once you reached 10.'

So they tried out Mark's suggestion, successfully locating a '.' after 10, pressing the second button. They then pressed out the sequence 1.618, and heard a distinct clicking sound. They were then able to separate to the two halves of the wooden container. An amazing sight met their eyes. There in front of them was a fine painting, a representation of the Annunciation. Alan, who was something of an art expert, responded.

'This could be by Botticelli or Fra Angelico, you know. We need to send this up to one of the big auction houses in London for a more expert opinion.'

What was the significance of that number sequence that had unlocked the secret of the painting's protective cover?

Less than a week later, they received a letter which suggested that the painting was probably by Botticelli or a pupil, and was very valuable. The significance of the number sequence was that the painting illustrated what is known as 'The Golden Section' in which the larger part of the picture is 1.618 times that of the lesser section.

Interestingly, a few months later, the painting sold for the sum of £1.618 million pounds.

A wilful harmonium

St. Aidan's had a comprehensive 'make-over' just five years ago. The old pews were removed and were replaced by something approaching more comfortable seating. The vestibule was made more welcoming, with glass frontage instead of the austere and rotting timber doors and their revolting dirty yellow paint. The old organ had long since gone – a Blackett and Howden which was not 'top of the range' when it was originally installed in 1928 and its pneumatic action so badly deteriorated that it had become unplayable. People were pleased with the new Johannus instrument, though some of the less well-informed asked crass questions like "Where are the pipes?" or "Is the blower where the old one was?".

A few items survived the 'modernisation': memorial plaques to past worthies, an original lectern, and a wooden pulpit which some thought was a fine piece of furniture and others thought was the most hideous monstrosity ever carved by human hands. Additionally, on the wall on the vestibule, was an old photograph, dating from 1902. It was a picture of a group of church members, all with severe facial expressions as if afflicted with chronic constipation.

Less noticeable, because tucked away in a corner and gathering dust, was an old harmonium. Manufactured by Tryber and Sweetland and dated 1892, it had been silent for a very long time. In fact, no presently living church member could recall its having ever been played. Perhaps one reason for its retention was its having belonged to the late Elsie Maybury. (It had belonged to her parents and had come with her when she joined the church more than 50 years ago.) Some people joked that if anyone dared to try and dispose of it, they would be struck down like Uzza.

The organist, John Travers, was of the view that, if it was to be kept, then it might at least be worth examining to ascertain its condition, and possibly restore it. He was eager to try out works for harmonium by the likes of Franck and Vierne. There was a retired engineer in the congregation, who loved tinkering with all manner of exotic and not so exotic machines, and was game to try and get this ancient gizmo going. Fred Hook would need Travers' restraining hand.

Surprisingly, they found that the bellows were intact. As for the cabinet of the instrument, there was a lot of dirt to be removed, including, of all things, mouse droppings. There was a small amount of woodworm, but it had not been too invasive and was easily remedied. With one exception, the reeds were also intact, and there were two stops that required repair, but all in all, the instrument wore its age well. John Travers contacted his friend Raymond Marsh, who worked for the local organ builders to get his opinion on the state of the instrument. Travers was itching to put it through its paces, although having said that, he had a recollection of playing a harmonium in a village chapel some years ago, which left him feeling as if his legs had been reduced to aching jelly. He was hoping for a pleasanter experience this time.

He thought he would have his first try one evening when there was no-one else in the church. He sat and tried out a few notes, getting used to the pedals operating the bellows. They were reasonably responsive, and promised the absence of agonising after effects. He had brought his copy of Franck's 'L'Organiste' with him. He picked 'An old carol' and set himself to play. He pressed the keys, he pumped strenuously, but absolutely nothing happened. He tried again. No sounds came. He then thought he would just try and improvise. Suddenly he found his hands were out of his control, and he was playing 'What a friend we have in Jesus'. After being compelled as if by an unseen force to play several verses, he then found himself playing 'The Old Rugged Cross'.

If there were two hymns calculated to make his toes curl, it was these. To have his hands made to play them was not his idea of fun. He made a special effort to withdraw his hands from the keyboard. He went and sat down on a chair nearby, trying to come to terms with what had just taken place. But there was more to come.

As he sat there, he witnessed the most amazing sight. The harmonium struck up again – this time with 'Abide with me'. Only this time, someone else was playing. There, on the stool, sat an elderly gentleman, suited and with an old fashioned collar and tie, playing away zealously. But he was not alone. He was surrounded by a number of other people, men and women in what looked like Victorian or Edwardian garments, and for all the world resembling the people in the photograph in the church vestibule! He sank back further into his chair. After a short while, the vision went, and he was once again alone in the church. What was he to make of this? An instrument that ruthlessly refused to play anything but the most limited repertoire, including things that he would only play reluctantly, and then only if he were paid to do so – like weddings and funerals. After all his efforts, was the instrument destined to once more stay unplayed in a corner, gathering dust? Was the late Elsie Maybury exerting a posthumous influence? As to the strange vision, John travers ascertained that the old gentleman playing was Elsie Maybury's father, and some of the other people in the photograph were also members of the family.

Boy with a tin whistle

I was returning home after a visit to Ireland. I had stayed at Waterford and Cork and seen the famous Lakes of Killarney. While I was away, I happened to be out in the country enjoying a pint of Guinness and looking out over the calm countryside. It was on this occasion that I had my first experience of seeing the boy with the tin whistle. To begin with, there was nothing to see. I heard the sound of a light wind instrument and a tune which I subsequently found out had the title 'The old woman from Wexford'. It was a lively tune in 6/8 time and I wondered where the sound was coming from. After a few moments I glanced behind me at a field containing tall grass and wild flowers. Then I saw him. He was striding through the meadow playing his whistle and started skipping along in time to the music. I stared at him and he stopped playing. I waved to him and put my hands together in a gesture of applause. Then to my amazement he just disappeared.

No-one else sitting outside the pub seemed to have seen or heard anything. When I mentioned it to the publican, he gave me a knowing wink and said rather flippantly that I must have overdone the Guinness or else been 'spelled' by the 'little people'. I didn't know how to react to this facetious, almost dismissive comment, but I reflected that it would sound odd telling folk about young whistle players who disappeared into thin air in broad daylight without anyone else noticing!

So there I was on the train from Cork to Rosslare to take the ferry over to Fishguard. We had all piled into the train which was quite crowded except for a few seats. Across from me were four seats with a table. Two seats on one side were occupied by a couple who sounded as if they came from Birmingham – Midlands anyway. I started to read my newspaper but came over feeling a little drowsy.

Then I heard the whistle again. This time I recognised the tune, 'The rocky road to Dublin'. As before, there was initially just the music and nothing to be seen. Then, in one of the empty seats opposite the couple the young lad gradually appeared and continued to play. But nobody else seemed to notice any of this. The young lad stopped playing and smiled. I found myself stammering out a question. 'Who are you?' The other folk round me stared, as well they might, since as far as they were concerned, I was addressing empty space. After another minute, the boy faded away, rather as he had done in the field.

We arrived in Rosslare. There was something of a scrum on the quayside, but we eventually got on board the ferry and I managed to find a comfortable lounge seat on the middle deck. We had a calm crossing. An hour or so into the journey, I thought I would go out outside for some fresh air and a walk from bow to stern. We were accompanied by gulls, some of them with aggressive intentions toward passengers who were desperately protecting their sandwiches and soft fruit.

As I walked along the deck, I heard that whistle again. Another tune, 'The Irish washerwoman' a lively jig that I had heard in a pub in Cork. There, leaning against the rail at the stern, was the young minstrel. I strode towards him, and as I got closer I asked him in a whisper 'where are you going?' he gestured across the water toward our destination. Then he was gone.

There was one more sighting on the way home. As I was leaving the train at Bristol to catch the bus, I saw him some way up the platform with his whistle. He waved, but then I lost him in the crowd. I got home and unpacked, and tried to make sense of my experiences. The youngster seemed to have followed me all the way from Waterford to Bristol. But why? I began to have dreams, which were essentially 're-runs' of the events. Gradually, over the weeks, these became less frequent and I ceased to think much about them. Until, that is, this morning.

I came down to find a book lying open on my desk in the study. I didn't recall taking it off the shelf. It was open at a page opposite a photo of a mansion. The book was about 18th century architecture and was open at a section on Furleigh House, just a few miles away. I had intended to visit it, along with some of the other 'stately homes' featured in the book. Furleigh had some fine furniture and paintings, and I decided to go there the following week.

It was just a short ride from Gloucester, out past some villages. When I arrived, there were already quite a number of visitors and tourists in a queue outside. They were only admitting groups of ten at a time, and I was waiting nearly half an hour before my group were able to enter the main hallway. Our guide took us round the larger rooms, pointing out the items of interest: some fine Flemish tapestries, some Delft ware, elegant silver pieces on the table in the dining-room. There were fine cabinets and corner tables, all inlaid. We passed along a broad landing with paintings and marble sculptures. Then there was a narrow corridor between the principal bedrooms. We were ushered through this fairly quickly, but I managed to lag behind the rest of the group because something caught my eye.

There were a few small pictures on the wall of the corridor, rural scenes and one picture of the house itself as it looked soon after it was first built. But there was one larger painting in the most dimly lit part of the corridor. I stared at it with something close to disbelief. It was a portrait, and it was a portrait of the young lad, dressed exactly as I had seen him before, and holding his tin whistle.

I caught with the rest of the group, and after the end of the tour of the house, I took the guide on one side and asked her about the picture I had just seen.

'Ah', she said. 'There's a story there. He was a poor orphan boy who was brought over here by the original owner of this house and was employed, along with some other musicians, in entertaining the guests. Sadly, he died young – he was only 16. He's buried in the graveyard of the estate chapel, a rare honour for one of such humble origins. But apparently the lady of the house was very fond of him, so that might explain it. It is said that he was always homesick and wished someone could take him back to Ireland. I believe his parents are buried somewhere in Waterford. Our nickname for him, unsurprisingly, is 'Paddy', but his real name was Joseph O'Malley.'

That is my name, too.

Cancelled

The Macfarlane Hall is an imposing edifice, though it must be said that it is not so much an aesthetic contribution to architecture as it is a monument to the industrialist whose name it bears. For capacity it dwarfs the town hall and the largest church, St. Matthews, situated on the town square. For this reason, it is the main concert venue, with a capacity of 2000. It also has a fine Harrison & Harrison organ mounted on a balcony at one end. It is too large for more intimate musical events which are held in the church or the Monteverdi Arts centre. For some years, regular organ recitals have been held, shorter ones at lunchtimes every Friday performed mainly by local organists, and the longer evening ones by international artists every two months. All these have been arranged by Ronald Cant and Thomas Phelps, who founded the Bradcaster Organ Society nearly two decades ago. The latest item on the schedule of events was to be a lunchtime recital by Edvard Lindemann, with a programme of music including works by Franck and Mendelssohn. Lindemann was a frequent visitor to Bradcaster, so people were looking forward to his performance.

Thomas Phelps had been in touch with Edvard Lindemann in the days before the visit to confirm arrangements. He would be travelling up the day before, staying overnight in the Clarendon Hotel in the town centre. He would then have a practice session in the morning, followed by a light early lunch before the recital at 1.15. He said he would be travelling alone this time, because his wife Dorte had a bad cold, and being asthmatic, felt it would not be wise for her to come. He would drive to the Park and Ride at his local station at Fenby and take the train from there.

At about 9.30 that evening, Thomas Phelps thought he would phone Edvard Lindemann, to check a few details. He had already received the list of items on the programme, and copies had already been printed for distribution the following day. He expected that Lindemann would have checked in and had an evening meal by then, so felt it would be a suitable time to discuss matters. However, when he rang the hotel, the receptionist reported that 'Mr Lindemann' had not yet arrived, and had not phoned to indicate that he would be late, or when he might arrive. Thomas waited for another hour and phoned the hotel a second time. Again, there had been no sign of Lindemann.

Maybe the train had been delayed, but then surely Lindemann might have phoned either the hotel or Thomas himself to say so? But there had been nothing. Nothing at all. Thomas eventually decided to phone his home at Fenby. Dorte answered, sounding a little hoarse and out of breath. She confirmed that Edvard had set out as planned at 2.00 p.m. to catch the 2.20 train, which should have arrived at 4.30. She said she would try phoning his mobile. But she later reported to Thomas that his phone was off. Both she and Thomas were starting to grow anxious. Had Edvard been in an accident? Wouldn't the emergency services have been in touch? For now, there was just an uneasy silence. Thomas was having to contemplate cancelling the recital and arranging refunds for those who had purchased tickets in advance.

At 7.00 a.m. the following morning, a member of station staff at Fenby noticed a silver BMW parked at the far end of the station car park. In it he found the body of a man slumped across the driver and passenger front seats of the vehicle. There was a lot of blood from what appeared to be a wound to the chest. The police arrived and the DVLA confirmed that the car (with a 'cherished' number-plate ED60 LDM) belonged to an Edvard Lindemann. Contents of a wallet found in the deceased's jacket identified the body as Lindemann's. Theft could hardly have been a motive since the wallet contained £75 in banknotes. On the back seat, there was a large travel bag which looked as if it had been emptied, sorted through and its contents roughly stuffed back into it. A set of car keys was found next to it. It was assumed that the bag had been in the boot. But why had it been sorted through? What had merited such attention?

It was quickly determined that the victim had died from a single gunshot to the chest, at close range. Since the car windows were intact, the thinking was that the killer must have opened the driver's door, or that Lindemann himself had perhaps opened the window. The pathologist arrived, and after preliminary examination, the body was removed. It now remained to carry out the unpleasant task of informing Dorte of her husband's death.

Dorte sat stunned on the sofa in the lounge. A WPC sat with her, comforting her while Inspector Paul

Crotch asked questions calmly and sensitively. She confirmed the details of his departure, the fact that Edvard's phone was off, she couldn't imagine what could possibly be of interest in his travel bag, which only contained his best suit for performing and other items sufficient for an overnight stay. She was told that no phone was found on the body or elsewhere in the car. She said he had also taken his laptop with him. Paul Crotch said there was no such item found at the scene. She couldn't understand why anyone would take it – it was an old machine, with just a few files of musical items. Hardly something to kill for. She was totally bewildered.

A good neighbour offered to come and stay in the house with her, and the WPC would be in regular contact at least once a day. Dorte asked that Thomas Phelps be informed. She would try and muster the courage to contact Edvard's relatives in Bergen, and also speak to her sister in Esbjerg, Denmark.

Thomas and Ronald could scarcely believe what they were told about Edvard. Down the years, they had had occasion to cancel recitals for various reasons – recitalist illness, fogbound airports, recalcitrant organ ciphers, etc. But not because of a murder. Why would anyone want to kill Edvard Lindemann?

So Thomas duly went ahead, and arranged for large notices to be put up in the entrance to the Macfarlane Hall advertising the cancellation of the recital. Subsequently, obituaries would be published in some of the major music journals and one or two 'quality' daily papers. But for most people his death remained an enigma. Dorte wondered whether Edvard's funeral should be held in Bergen, but his relatives were prepared to come over, as was her sister Birgitte. There was an inquest with the verdict of unlawful killing by person or persons unknown. This was, needless to say, frustrating and unsatisfactory.

Unsatisfactory for Paul Crotch and his team. He was determined to track down the killer, although there were no immediate lines of inquiry. Nothing had been found at the crime scene. Whoever had carried out the killing had been meticulous, this had been a professional 'hit' and not an opportunist theft gone wrong. No fingerprints, no DNA, no spent bullet case. The killer had probably used a silencer. Crotch had set up an incident room and the team were all set to launch into a full scale investigation.

Until, that is, on the first day of planning, a constable from the station reception desk came upstairs and whispered in Crotch's ear. There were two 'suits' downstairs asking to see the head of the team. The two 'suits' came up and Crotch invited them into his office. They were together for some time. Other officers were wondering what was going on.

'Who are these goons?' one of them asked.

Nobody had a clue. After an hour, the 'suits' or 'goons' emerged poker-faced and took their leave. Crotch was very subdued, as if all his energy and enthusiasm had ebbed away.

'Sorry, everybody. The game's off. We've had 'orders' from on high to cease the investigation. It's out of our hands now, I'm afraid. Sorry I'm not even at liberty to answer any questions. I know that must piss you off as much as it does me. But I don't know what the hell's going on, and it looks like it wouldn't be healthy to speculate further or blab about this outside this room, OK?'

A few grunts and grumbles followed, and everyone turned their attention to other crimes.

The 'suits' who didn't even disclose their names, were members of the security services. This was now their case. The likes of Thomas and Ronald, Paul Crotch and even Dorte herself were destined to be shut out of a darker world. This didn't stop Dorte indulging in her own speculation. Had Edvard been involved in some clandestine activity? Had he led a double life? As an international performer, he had been accustomed to travelling across continents – Europe, the USA, even South America. Had he got involved in drugs trafficking? Surely not. But why had he been killed? She was still puzzled as to why his laptop and phone had been so significant to the anonymous assassin. Why had the local police closed down their investigation? The WPC who had looked after her since Edward's death understood her predicament but said that she was 'under orders' not to discuss the matter. Off the record, however, she hinted that the case had been taken over by 'higher authority'.

Dorte needed a change of scene. She had no plans to move. She and Edvard had settled in the UK some years ago. But neither Norway nor Denmark were far away, so she would be able to visit his relatives and her sister too on a regular basis. So after a few weeks, she set off to spend a week in Esbjerg.

What she did not know was that while she was away, there was a development in the case which was part of the 'hush-hush' surrounding Edvard's murder. A residential block in Croydon houses a variety of tenants. Some of these are immigrants, for others it is a temporary accommodation for single mothers and children. Then there are various individual tenants. Unemployed artists and musicians, and the almost inevitable drug addicts and prostitutes. But on one day, it was flat 27 that became the object of attention. A white van drove up to the apartment block. Four men in dark clothes and wearing balaclavas burst into the flat. They were there to arrest someone known locally as Dan Kaminski. There was a shoot-out and the 'target' was fatally wounded. He was in fact Gregor Borev, born in Bulgaria but since childhood a Russian citizen. In the flat, they found Lindemann's lap-top and mobile phone and a variety of 'sensitive' items connecting Borev with Russian Intelligence operatives. Borev's own phone contained a large number of cryptic or coded text messages. One of the more recent of these was a terse two-word text – Lindemann's name followed by a Russian word which translates as 'wiped out' or 'cancelled'.

Cindy and Burney

Cindy lost her dad when she was only six. A car crash involving a drunken lout taking a blind bend too quickly, resulting in a head-on collision. Her dad had been organist at the local church for a number of years and the rest of the family were quite musical as well. Her mum was a violinist and taught at the local secondary school. Her aunt was a clarinettist and played for a local amateur orchestra. Cindy loved hearing her father play and had hoped that, one day, he would teach her the rudiments of the instrument. There was a baby grand in the lounge at home and Cindy also had a keyboard in her bedroom. This was a good quality instrument of its type and had been chosen by her father, who, not surprisingly, was rather sniffy about some of the 'cheap plastic gizmos polluting the market', as he once put it. 'Cheap gadgets for the musically challenged' was another of his phrases.

Cindy's bedroom was small, and a little cluttered. The keyboard was positioned under the window. In the daytime, her bed was covered with a variety of soft toys – with one exception – a rather large teddy-bear, perched, rather than seated, in a little doll's chair by the door. He was at this time as big as Cindy herself. He was a golden brown colour, smartly got up in a highly decorated waistcoat and blue trousers, with a musical patterned bow tie. Her father had bought him as a Christmas present, christening him 'Burney'. He explained to Cindy that 'Burney' was the name of an 18th century English composer and organist. Cindy also learned that he was the father of Fanny Burney who wrote 'naughty books' she would find out about when she was older. (She recalled her father having a mischievous twinkle in his eye, when imparting this morsel of information. She was not brought up in a climate of prudery!)

Cindy began to wonder whether she would ever get to learn the organ now her father was no longer there. He had promised that, one day, he would start to give her some preliminary tuition. She was a little frustrated anyway, because she had not grown sufficiently for her feet to reach the pedals. She felt nervous at the idea of approaching the new organist at the church. Initially, she was likely to find it emotionally difficult seeing someone else playing the instrument. While she was musing about this, looking out of her bedroom window, she started muttering – talking to herself, as imaginative children often do.

'I wonder what I could play, even if I can't use my feet?' she sighed.

'Oh, don't you worry about that', said a deep voice from behind her. Cindy was startled. That voice had made her jump. Then she turned round. There was Burney sitting upright, twiddling his bow tie.

'Yes, my dear, there's plenty you could try playing even now – what are you – nearly seven? Perhaps you don't realise it, but nearly half the organ music ever written doesn't have a pedal part, and some of it is quite good stuff I assure you – elegant and exquisite.'

Cindy gasped and sat amazed at Burney's almost fatherly – or should one say, grandfatherly, demeanour.

Cindy reflected for a moment.

'Do you mean I could try some of these pieces on this keyboard?', she asked.

'Of course', Burney replied.

'Your father wisely chose one with several organ type settings – enough to mimic changes of registration between movements. (He had to explain some of these technicalities, but Cindy was bright and caught on very quickly.) You will see all this when you next visit the instrument in the church – all the stops to choose from. You may be familiar with some of this already, because you sometimes sat on the bench with your father while he was practising.'

Cindy wondered what she might try and play to get started.

'Well, my dear', said Burney, 'how about asking your mother if you could look through some of your father's music. I suggest you look for 'manuals only' pieces. You're bound to find some. Collections of voluntaries by 18th century composers – look out for names like James, Stanley, Walond or Prelleur. No shortage of material. Take care though. Some of it is more difficulty and fiddly than you might think!'

Cindy's head was spinning. She thanked Burney and went downstairs. Her mother was in the lounge.

'Mum! Do you think I could have a look at some of Dad's music?' she asked. Her mother raised an eyebrow.

'What are you looking for, Cindy?" she asked.

'Well...er, voluntaries...by 18th century composers like er... Stanley...'

Her mother's eyebrows rose higher.

'Good lord, how do you know all that?', was her response. She then directed Cindy to the large bookcase at the end of the lounge. Two whole shelves were taken up with musical scores of one kind or another, so she had to rummage around. She became absorbed in the contents of the shelves, as if she were a much younger child in a toy shop. She finally settled on a set of slim volumes of Old English Organ music edited by someone called C. H. Trevor.

'How about these?' she asked Burney, on returning to her bedroom.

'Some of these should do', he replied, looking through the volumes.

'Well. What do you know, there's even a fugue by my namesake.' This made Burney chuckle. He turned a few more pages.

'I would recommend you start with some of the slow movements' he advised. 'However, don't overdo the 'Adagio' thing. It doesn't mean you have to play as if you're trying to send yourself and everyone else into a deep coma. These pieces have a natural pulse, you know. When you come to the Vivace movements, you don't rush frantically through them like your knickers are on fire!' This made Cindy snigger out loud.

She spent some hours in her room practising with the volume turned down. She was getting the 'feel' for this type of music, and began to recall her father playing some of it at the end of church services. When she emerged later for her tea, her mother stared at her intently.

'Was that really you playing? I thought you might be playing one of Dad's CDs and you seemed to be talking to yourself a lot.'

Afterwards, Cindy went back upstairs and reported her mother's remarks to Burney.

'You will go far, my dear. Just keep practising and one day you will progress to use of the pedals.'

Burney's prophecy proved correct. So well did she progress that, when she was ten, the new church organist allowed her to deputise for him when he was away. Later, she took music through school and on to university. Now, aged twenty-two, she is entering for her ARCO. Burney still occupies pride of place in her new flat that she shares with her boyfriend. He will perhaps never know how much she owes to the bear with the musical bow tie!

Console gremlins

The church of St. Mary's-in-the-Marsh is a small building, predominantly Norman with a few later additions. It occupies a central position in the village of Little Fenbury, overlooking The Green. It has a fine lych-gate, and the small graveyard is well looked after. Inside, there is a board listing all the clergy who have served as vicars since the 16th century, as well as the expected memorials to all and sundry. The altar has a fine reredos, surprisingly ornate.

The church also sports a Vowles organ, sadly past its best. One might say the same, regrettably, about the organist, David Boyce, who in recent years has shown a greater leaning toward inebriation as opposed to improvisation. However, he still jealously guarded his stewardship of the instrument and the vicar, the Rev. John Keeble, studiously avoided confrontation with him, settling for minimal communication over choice of hymns, offertory pieces and psalms. The congregation were used to Boyce: many of them were among his contemporaries and hardly remember anyone else occupying the organ bench. Which didn't stop them moaning, of course. (This was, for some of them, part of a Sunday morning's recreation; that is, when they were not nodding off during the sermon!)

Returning to the matter of inebriation...

Boyce was in The Coachman pub, imbibing as usual, or should one say, more than usual. The landlord,

John Reading, was trying to drop none too gentle hints to Boyce that perhaps it was time to finish and go home. Boyce responded with something slurred and unintelligible, but nonetheless managed to stagger out of the pub and lurch up the street.

For some reason best known to himself, he took a notion to enter the church on his way home. He swayed his way through the churchyard, nearly tripping over a low gravestone as he went, sending a small vase of flowers flying into the long grass. He blundered into, rather than opened, the door, and then meandered up the aisle to the chancel. The organ was positioned on the south wall, not that Boyce would have been able to tell south from north at this point, but he nonetheless scrambled on to the organ bench and managed to maintain an upright posture, staring blearily into the mirror above the console. He fumbled around for a moment, switching on the instrument and drawing a few stops, rummaging through a disorganised pile of music, some of it so dog-eared you might have thought the mice had been at it. He was about to select a piece when something caught his attention.

In turning round on the bench, he had inadvertently depressed a key on the Great with his elbow. Annoyingly, the note continued to play even after he had lifted his arm. He muttered an expletive under his breath, and fiddled around trying to stop the cipher. Then, right in front of him, standing on the key was a little gremlin figure with a scowl on its face.

'Wotcha!', the gremlin said in a gruff voice.

'What the ****?!' was Boyce's response. Alcohol increased his fluency with Anglo-Saxon.

Somehow, through the haze in his brain, he had registered that this strange dwarf was responsible for the cipher.

'We ain't finished yet, not by long chalks, mister!', the gremlin continued.

'We?' mused Boyce, swaying in his seat.

Then, from the side of the console out trooped half a dozen more gremlins like the first one. They all stood in a line with sinister grins on their faces. The first one said,

'OK, guys, let's give him a burst of the ole sing-song.'

At which point, they all began to sing, horribly out of tune, belting out the following lyric:

'We are the cipher gremlins, naughty girls and boys. There's nothing we like better than to cause unwanted noise!'

Then they all collapsed in heaps of laughter and danced up and down on the keys, causing further cacophony in the process. Then they climbed up and sat down in a row on the keys of the Swell manual. The ciphers ceased. Boyce prodded the keys on the Great. Nothing. No sound could be produced from any of the keys, regardless of which stops were drawn. Then, from behind the stop jamb on the other side of the organ emerged another group of gremlins with glum expressions carrying cards. They lined themselves up on the great manual, arranging themselves so that the cards now read:

'We are the nifty gliders, seizing up the wooden sliders. Making mischief all around, making sure there's not a sound!'

These gremlins then appeared to be chuckling, but without making a sound. They sat down on the Great keys and glared at Boyce. He shifted about on the bench and his left foot accidentally depressed a low note on the pedals. A guttural sound resulted and persisted, so unpleasant that he tried to cover his ears to shut out the noise. Then from below there emerged a considerably larger gremlin, more menacing than any of the others.

'OK, you', he said loudly and rudely above the pedal noise. 'Allow me to introduce meself. I am the Chief Buggerator.

Boyce timidly asked, 'What?'

The gremlin replied, 'I am in charge of all the buggeration in this instrument, and there's nothing you can do about it, right?'

Boyce was by this time reeling with a combination of alcoholic haze and incredulity. The large gremlin ended his discourse with lyrics of his own:

'I love to mess things up before they really start. There is no greater fun than to make a pedal fart!'

All this was too much for Boyce. He swooned and fell forwards. The gremlins all rushed away out of sight.

This was the way he was found the following day, sprawled over the manuals, snoring very loudly. He had to be assisted off the bench and helped to walk home. He was never quite the same afterwards, and never played again. A young graduate, Alan Best, took over for a period before he departed for Durham to pursue research. As for the Vowles, it rapidly ceased to function, although many members of the congregation were concerned about the cost of its removal. The gremlins had won the day.

Diabolus in musica

Ronald Goodwin was much respected in the village. Along with his long-term partner, Fiona Hine, he had made a major contribution to the musical life of the community. He was organist and choirmaster at St. Luke's and arranged concerts and festivals which drew in people from far and wide. As autumn approached, he was engaged in lengthy practice and rehearsals, encouraging the modest choir of twenty-two to take on a performance of Messiah. The village was lucky in having a reasonable complement of male singers, often a problem for choirs these days.

So it was, one sunny October afternoon, Ronald Goodwin set out from the cottage he and Fiona had occupied for nearly twenty years. His accustomed route took him through the centre of the village, past The Falconer's Arms and the general store (the only surviving shop), past the old water pump and the small war memorial on the central green. Several of the locals greeted him and he waved back at them.

Ronald Goodwin never made it to the church. When he failed to return home in the evening, Fiona tried to contact him on his mobile, but got no reply. She went out into the village asking people if they had seen Ronald earlier on his way to the church. Some of them had, but no-one had seen him during the latter part of the afternoon. Fiona rang the vicar, the Rev. David Alcock, but he had not seen him at the church and Alcock had found the building empty in the middle of the afternoon.

St. Luke's churchyard is quite small. There are some old graves dating back to the early 18th century, but very few new ones, these latter being family plots still maintained by relatives. The graveyard peters out in an area of long grass below a line a yew trees, and a small side gate leads out into a cornfield belonging to a nearby farm. The long grass was concealing a horror that was to destroy the previously gentle calm of the village.

Jocelyn Heron was in the habit of walking her golden retriever 'Russ' through the village, cutting through the churchyard and following a path round the cornfield to the old mill behind the farm. However, on this occasion, Russ was noticeably sniffing round the long grass near the side gate. Jocelyn tried to draw him away, regretting having let him off the lead. But he would not respond to the call to move on, so she walked over to the spot where he was sniffing and making an unusual whimpering sound. It was then that she saw what was engaging Russ' attention. There, lying in the grass, was the body of Ronald Goodwin, covered in blood from what appeared to be multiple stab wounds, mainly in the chest, but also in the neck. Ronald Goodwin had been the victim of a brutal and frenzied attack.

The local community were scarcely able to believe what had happened. The police had no obvious leads. Everybody in the village was interviewed as a matter of course. Particular attention was given to the congregation, though hardly anyone thought one of them could have done anything so dreadful. Certain questions arose: had there been any people attending St. Luke's who were not 'regulars'?

Well, one whose attendance was erratic was old Marty Long, but he was so frequently 'under the influence' he would have been in no state to stab anything or anybody. There were occasional visitors, of course. One week there had been some Canadians looking up ancestors in old parish records; one or two vagrants sleeping rough in the churchyard from time to time, but not aggressive or threatening. Rev. Alcock often managed to find hostel accommodation for these people.

However, the police began to find a convergence in the witness accounts relating to one young man who sometimes visited the church, but not necessarily on Sundays. Ronald Goodwin had himself reported that on one occasion while he was practising, the youth had, for no apparent reason run screaming from the church. Some members of the congregation had teased Ronald about this.

'Didn't think your playing was that bad, Ronald!', one of them said jokingly.

But what was the explanation of the young man's extraordinary behaviour?

All that most people knew was that his name was Rick. Subsequently it was learned that his name was Stubley and that he originally came from somewhere in Hampshire. Beyond that, not much more was known. He was usually rather quiet and withdrawn, which made his dramatic outburst all the more alarming. The police finally caught up with him living in the same hostel as Marty Long, although it appeared that they had little or nothing to do with one another.

When interviewed, Stubley was not altogether coherent, and exhibited a nervous tic. Further investigation revealed that he had ongoing mental health issues but was on medication, and was being monitored to keep track of his condition. He had had a disturbed history. He had had violent episodes when he was younger, on one occasion stabbing his mother while she was playing the piano. She was a talented pianist, but sadly she had died of cancer when she was only 42 and he was just 16. But what had triggered the attack on his own mother?

Rick was himself quite musical although he didn't play an instrument. He had, however developed an unhealthy interest in Satanism, an interest which persisted into the present despite attempts to wean him off it. The police found all manner of literature, posters, CDs and computer games involving devil-worship and bloody sacrifice. He was apparently quite sensitive to sound and especially certain kinds of dissonance. If he heard certain chords, he could become highly agitated, and it was the effect of the piece his mother was playing that triggered his violence against her.

The police called a psychiatrist, Dr. Mark Stafford Smith, who had first diagnosed Rick's condition. He found that certain music had to be avoided, otherwise Rick could go berserk. There had been occasions on which he had had to be physically restrained. Stafford Smith had performed some tests to ascertain the specific type of musical trigger that affected Rick. He asked to sit in on the interviews conducted by the police.

Rick was a little surprised to see his psychiatrist there, but ii seemed to calm him down, initially. Stafford

Smith had a small tape machine which he placed on the interview table. He addressed the two officers present.

'I am going to play this very brief tape.'

He pressed the 'play' button. Suddenly, Rick jumped up and tried to grab one of the officers by the throat with the result that they both ended up on the floor. Stafford Smith quickly injected Rick with a sedative.

'I'm sorry about that', he said. 'That was worse than I was expecting.'

One officer began swearing,

'What the fuck do you think you were playing at?'

Stafford Smith did his best to calm things down. Rick was now quiet and passive on his chair.

'I don't want to bore your socks off gentlemen, but what I played was a sequence of chords known as 'tritones' – chords with three full tones. The first one was C – F sharp, the second A – E flat, and so on. They are harsh and uncomfortable sounds. There is a story that in mediaeval times such chords were banned as 'Diabolus in Musica' or 'The Devil in Music'. It is possible that Rick had heard Mr Goodwin playing a piece or pieces involving tritones as a conspicuous feature. What we do know is that his mother was playing a piano version of 'Danse Macabre' by Saint-Saens when he stabbed her.'

This left the police with the bizarre explanation that the devil in Rick had been released by the devil in the music to which he had been exposed.

Hillfire

'Bloody hell! Not again!'

She looked out of the window at the back of her bungalow. The hill behind was once again ablaze. Members of the local brigade were desperately working to control the spread of the flames which were rapidly consuming the dry grass and gorse. It was almost certain that the fire had been started deliberately, like the previous one a month earlier. The culprits in that case had been caught, but it seemed that there was no shortage of morons with pyromania.

Vivienne Lascelles was especially anxious. Last time, but for a change of wind direction, she might have had to move out of her home, with little time to pick up just a few belongings. This would have meant potential loss of more valuable items. As a concert pianist, Vivienne cherished her Steinway grand and the many files of music scores and recordings she had accumulated over the years. Insurance cover does not really compensate for losses of this sort.

She was expecting a visit from members of the fire crew at any moment. More or less on cue, there was a ring of the bell.

'Morning madam. You hardly need telling about the fire. We're here to warn you that you might well have to evacuate your home, so make sure you have a bag packed ready to leave. We've already moved out the folks on The Row into the community centre at Mayfield.'

The Row was the local name for a set of cottages officially called Oakey Terrace. Vivienne knew some of the people from The Row. Some of them belonged to a walking club that regularly rambled over the local hills. Vivienne very occasionally joined the group when she was home from her concert trips. One person in particular, Lynette Kirby, was an amateur violinist, and she and Vivienne sometimes played together when time permitted. Lynette was in a relationship with another 'Row' resident, Richard Bailey, who owned a chemist's in Mayfield.

What was not widely known was that Vivienne was herself in a relationship with both Lynette and Richard. Vivienne was quite relaxed about this – OK, so she liked the girls as well as the boys, so what? (She still retained a North country bluntness of attitude.) The tricky part of all of this was that Lynette had a rather controlling and at times abusive partner Craig, and she suspected that she and Richard were being followed or watched by him, although she could not be certain.

There was a further complication. Richard had an ex-partner Mylene, and continued to pester him and make threatening phone calls. Vivienne was glad to get away and become absorbed in her rehearsals and concert schedules.

She had a pre-arranged visit to the Barbican in London in a week's time to discuss rehearsals and programmes with the leader of the Harmonia Ensemble, David Le Maître. She was not sure about leaving home in the present circumstances, and was at the point of contacting him about a postponement when the bell rang again.

'Hello again', said the fire officer. 'I'm pleased to say that the fire is under control now, so you should be OK to stay where you are.'

She pointed out that she was proposing to be away at her flat in London for a few days, so she would leave her phone number with someone in case she needed to be contacted. She thought of either Richard or Lynette. She tried ringing them but got no reply. She tried several times over the next few days. This was puzzling to say the least.

She decided to go down to 'The Row' to see if either of them was at home. She knew that they sometimes went walking either alone or together on the hills nearby, but she hadn't seen them, as she sometimes did, from her rear window. She happened to meet a neighbour who said she hadn't seen either of them for days. Perhaps they had gone away. But it was a little surprising that at least one of them hadn't told her. They hadn't joined the others in the community centre. The neighbour said that everyone else was in the process of moving back now the danger was past. So where were they?

"In the wake of the recent hill fires near Mayfield, the badly charred remains of two people have been discovered in burned gorse bushes close to Meadow Brook. The identity of the persons concerned has yet to be established", said Detective Inspector Mark Rowlands, who is currently heading the investigation. "At present the cause of death is not known. This is Anita Workman for Radio MFC."

Vivienne sat stunned, almost spilling her coffee over her breakfast cereal. Once the imagination takes wing, you can fear anything. Was it Richard and Lynette, who got trapped in the conflagration? Surely they would have seen the fire developing and made a speedy escape. They had been missing for days. The fire had only started more recently. Vivienne was restless and uncertain whether she was in a fit state of mind to go to London after all. Another few days, or even a week would not make a lot of difference. David Le Maître would understand.

Well, she put off her London trip. She became more concerned when the police finally confirmed that they were now engaged in a murder inquiry. It emerged that that deceased pair had not died in the hill fire, but had been killed earlier and their bodies dumped in the undergrowth on the hill. The evidence was that the victims had been shot.

Vivienne was in turmoil. Who on earth would shoot Richard or Lynette? Would Lynette's husband go to such extremes? But this was all speculation.

After a while, Vivienne could no longer put off her London trip, and took the train to Paddington, indulging in the luxury of First Class. David met her and took her to the concert venue. They had a pleasant day with the other members of the Harmonia Ensemble. She decided to stay for a few days at her flat in Chelsea, do some initial rehearsals and initial outlines for future programmes. She and David also wanted to discuss recordings for some of the well-known labels.

While she was away, she heard no news about the police investigation. When she got back she learned, with some relief, that the bodies were those of two males in their twenties, and further information had come to light indicating that they were Romanian nationals and possibly associated with some mafia-style gang engaged in drugs and people trafficking. They may have been the victims of some gang feud, but it meant that they were dead before the fire broke out on the hill.

This still left the problem of the whereabouts of Richard and Lynette. There was no sign of them at The Row and the police had been unable to trace their movements during the preceding fortnight. Lynette didn't own a car (the only vehicle was Craig's and he would hardly allow her to use it.) But Richard's car was missing.

Both Craig and Mylene had been interviewed, and their own homes searched, but nothing of any significance had been found. Craig had admitted that he knew of Lynette's affair with Richard and was going to have a confrontation with them, but they both disappeared before he could carry out his threat. Mylene said she had been trying to phone Richard for days but got no answer, so she assumed he was away, possibly with Richard. Both Craig and Mylene remained on the suspects list, and Mark Rowlands wasn't finished with them yet. Neither had satisfactory alibis for the days following Richard and Lynette's disappearance, but there was no forensic evidence. In fact, Mark Rowlands and his team had yet to establish foul play as they had with the murdered Romanians.

Vivienne found it difficult to concentrate. She was in the habit of practising every day, and had a number of works to study and prepare, including the Mozart concerto K491 and several pieces by Fanny Mendelssohn. She would soon have to return to London. So she would have to try and get herself together in advance of what was to be a busy schedule, embracing trips abroad to Chicago and Berlin. She would be away for some time.

She asked one of the neighbours to keep an eye on the homes of the missing couple while she was away, and also to have a phone number so that she might be able to keep up with any developments. In a matter of weeks, she was in a plane for Berlin along with members of the Ensemble. At last she had something positive to focus her mind.

Mark Rowlands was also trying to focus his mind. Eventually, CCTV and other footage showed Richard's car entering the motorway at Mayfield. It was evening and the images were not clear enough to see the occupants other than to establish that there were two individuals, the driver and front seat passenger, both probably male, and both wearing dark glasses, with their coat collars pulled up. Much later the vehicle showed up in outer London. The last image was of the car turning off in the direction of a block of flats in Acton.

Rowlands contacted his colleagues in London. The following day, the police raided one of the flats and arrested two men, both Romanian. In one of the lock-up garages at the rear of the building they found Richard's car. The rear seats had been folded down and under a tarpaulin they found the bodies of Richard and Lynette. The men arrested initially pretended to have linguistic difficulties, but it quickly became obvious that they understood perfectly well when they were arrested and charged. They had been intending to dispose of the bodies the next day. Why had they killed Richard and Lynette? Because they had accidentally stumbled on the men killing their two fellow Romanians and dumping them on the hillside. The couple had tried to run away, but were caught as they reached Richard's car. He and Lynette had both been shot.

It took a long time for Vivienne to come to terms with what had happened. She had lost two of the people closest to her, not to jealous partners or ex-partners, but at the hands of murderous strangers.

Jerry Molto's magic one-man band

No-one was sure where Jerry Molto came from. By reputation he was given to spinning yarns and that included some about himself. According to one account, his grandparents came over on the 'Windrush' and settled initially in Wolverhampton. His parents had seven children and he was the next to youngest with only a sister, Sonya, below himself. But as for his post childhood life, not much was known.

Apparently, he had shown musical talent from an early age. Some school friends confirmed that he could play several instruments, but as far as anybody could make out, he had not had any formal tuition. After some years drifting in and out of employment in rather poorly paid menial jobs, he managed to land a spot playing with a band in one of the night clubs somewhere in the North East of England – Sunderland or Newcastle, some said. Somewhat surprisingly given his circumstances, he showed no evidence of alcohol or drug addiction, and was a relatively moderate smoker. Not that there was any shortage of smoke in most of the places he frequented in those days. As for the band (they called themselves 'The Swanee River Blues Band'), they consisted of Leroy (pianist), Ainsley (double bass), 'Kipper' (violin) and Frankie (percussion). Jerry mainly played trumpet or sax. For a while, they had a singer, Lola Mae, who could cover a wide repertoire from Bessie Smith to Billie Holiday and was a major 'draw' to the club. (Not just for her singing, but probably also because she sported a gown slit to the top of the thigh, with fine legs that 'started under her chin', as someone said.)

The club didn't survive a major police raid, and several members and the manager were arrested for drug trafficking and prostitution. Somehow, Jerry managed to escape suspicion, but he and the others were now out of a job. Lola was lucky. She was talent spotted and landed a regular slot in a superior club on the other side of town. Jerry was reduced to busking and temporary labouring jobs for a while, until one of his former contacts got him an introduction to the Cotton Club. (The name was meant to have ironic reference to slavery and the plantations, so it is said.)

Then things started to look up for Jerry. He had his own spot several nights a week. One night, he would play piano, another night he played sax or trumpet. On occasion, he would even entertain on the harmonica. He began to get a reputation and attracted the interest of the local media, including the local television network who sent someone to interview him.

Sometimes Jerry's gimmick was to start off with his small stage in total darkness, with even the 'house' lights dimmed as well. Then a light would be shone on one small area, revealing him standing, or else seated at the piano. As the evening progressed, the same device would be used. The lights would go out and the spot would come on showing him in a different part of the stage with a different instrument. This was a 'one-man band' with a difference. But the big surprise was yet to come.

Some Cotton Club regulars who had heard of Jerry's previous jobs, including the club where he had worked with 'The Swanee', wondered whether he would go back to working as part of a group, on the grounds that it might be less exhausting for Jerry himself. But there was next to no prospect of the original group reforming. Lola Mae was now something of a star and was recording for a well-known label. Frankie, sadly, had died of an overdose, and Kipper was serving time at Her Majesty's pleasure for fencing stolen goods. (He was however, entertaining his fellow inmates and the 'screws' as well.)

The club manager approached Jerry in the afternoon while he was rehearsing for his evening show, suggesting that he might consider trying to form a new group. The idea might take off and a new group might end up touring, not just round the local clubs, but more widely. Jerry greeted this suggestion with a smile and also something of a twinkle in his eye, as if he were about to perpetrate some mischief.

A fortnight later, the Cotton Club was even busier than usual for a Friday night. Things were quite lively and noisy, until, following Jerry's usual strategy, all the lights went out, and there was an excited hush with some low murmuring and one or two giggles.

Then, suddenly, the entire stage was flooded with light. There, front of stage, was Jerry, ready with his sax. There were four others on stage with him: one at the piano, one on double-bass, one on violin, and one on percussion – all very reminiscent of the 'Swanee' band. But there was one very strange difference. All the other players had full face masks.

The group went through their routine for nearly an hour, attracting great applause (and loud oral contributions from the more inebriated). Then at the end of the hour, all the other players removed their masks and there was a gasp from the audience. Each of those other players was the spitting image of Jerry himself!

Then all the lights went out, people were fumbling in the dark, reaching for their mobile phones for torches. There was quite a hub-bub until the lights came back on. Everyone looked at the stage. Jerry was lying on the floor. Of the other players there was nothing to be seen.

Several staff rushed forward to attend to Jerry, but it was too late. He seemed to have had a heart attack and died very quickly.

But where were the other players? Was it all an illusion, a trick with mirrors? It hardly seemed credible. The only thing they found on stage other than the instruments were four masks – masks with a sinister smile.

Lady Sarah's spinet

Bradleigh Lodge is a Georgian house set in typically English rural surroundings. Built in 1725, it is a modest if elegant residence, and one of several occupied from time to time by the family of Lady Sarah Whately. The principal withdrawing room has some fine furniture, and a sequence of large paintings – family members, including one of Sarah herself – the only known portrait in existence.

Just below her picture was a spinet, believed to have been made by Cawton Aston, with a beautifully inlaid case. It had been maintained in a playable condition for some years, although no present-day member of the family played it. Occasionally, distinguished visiting musicians were invited to play it at specially arranged 'soirees'.

As for Lady Sarah herself, it was almost her personal instrument and by all accounts she was an accomplished player. She was acquainted with the work of Elizabeth Turner (d.1756) and owned copies of some of her keyboard pieces. It is said that she composed some music herself, but nothing survives in the family archive. However, this loss was to pale into significance compared with what happened just three years ago.

It was decided that some restoration work should be undertaken in the main rooms. Some of the plaster, especially in the ceilings, had 'blown' and there had been damp penetration in the walls in the North-facing part of the house. The paintings themselves had not received much attention over the years, and they certainly needed careful cleaning. This could not be done in situ, so the entire collection had to be removed to the premises of a reputable conservator in London. The spinet had by this time not been played for a while, and disappointingly, it had deteriorated somewhat. But worse was to come.

All the paintings, some fifteen in all, were delivered to the workshops of Laurence Benedict. It was expected that the cleaning and repair to the canvases would take up to six months, which would be ample time for the room walls to be redecorated (including the regilding of the cornices and architraves)

The spinet was moved into a small dressing room until it could be taken away for skilled repair, although proper tuning would have to wait until it was returned to the Lodge.

A matter of a fortnight later, a fire broke out in the Benedict workshops in the very part where the most recent items had been stored on arrival. This included the painting collection from the Lodge. It took several appliances to bring the blaze under control, but unfortunately some of the stored items did not survive, including the portrait of Lady Sarah Whately. The present owner, Barbara Newcome- Prescott, a distant relative and descendent of another branch of the family, was shocked at the losses, but this was not to be the end of the disasters.

Just three weeks after the fire, a van from Barton & Hayward, the keyboard specialists, turned up at the Lodge. The driver, Terry Bayliss, had been detailed to pick up the spinet. He was without on his own, so it took two members of lodge staff to assist him in carefully wrapping the instrument in quilting and sacking and gently laying it on the van floor, anchoring it where possible to avoid any unwanted movement in transit. Barbara Newcome-Prescott phoned ahead to the office at Barton & Hayward, partly to complain about failure to send out assistance with the driver but also to stress the need for careful handling at the other end. Bayliss got into his van and drove off.

Barbara now thought she could concentrate on the ramifications of the fire and problems of insurance claims. Fortunately, some years previously, an inventory of the house contents had been made, hard bound, complete with colour plate photographs of the paintings and the spinet. A copy was also saved as a computer file.

Terry Bayliss was approaching the by-pass, not travelling particularly fast, and was nearing the bridge over the Wear when the most extraordinary thing happened. Suddenly, a woman rushed out into the road in front of him, raising an outstretched hand as if ordering him to stop. He took rapid action to avoid hitting her, but lost control of the vehicle and it plunged down the embankment by the bridge, rolling over once before coming to rest just short of the river.

Another driver, who saw the van leave the road, stopped and raced down the slope and helped Bayliss out of the van. But Bayliss could not walk – he had a broken leg and sore ribs, so his rescuer managed to help him part way up the embankment and then dialled 999. They had only just managed to put themselves at a sufficient distance from the van when it exploded into flames, producing a cloud of thick smoke that brought the traffic on the bridge to a standstill. Terry Bayliss passed out, and the next thing he knew was waking up in the ambulance, with a paramedic attending to him.

'Don't worry, mate, you'll be OK soon. Just relax and try and breathe slowly.'

Barbara was now confronted with the news that the spinet had been lost in another conflagration. She found it difficult understand how a woman could have appeared as from nowhere and caused such an accident. The police were puzzled too, and questioned Terry Bayliss as soon as the doctors thought he was fit enough, once his leg was in plaster.

He told them that a young woman had indeed rushed into the road in front of him, but had no idea what happened to her after that, because he was struggling with his van. He was amazed she hadn't been killed by other vehicles coming behind him. He was asked for a description of the woman. She was quite young – maybe in her twenties – but what he found odd was the way she was dressed. 'Like the olden days – long blue dress – low cut – big cleavage – great tits!' he said with some relish.

('No wonder he went off the road!', observed one of the officers.) However, although at first they had assumed he must have been 'under the influence', there was no trace of either drugs or alcohol in his system, and he had no history of hallucinations or other aberrations. There was no evidence that he had fallen asleep at the wheel. It was a case of 'just one of those things'.

Barbara Newcome-Prescott was not the sort of person to be fobbed off with a 'just one of those things' non-explanation. She had lost the one and only portrait of a female ancestor, and that ancestor's beloved instrument has also been reduced to ashes. She was determined to have a conversation with the young man Terry Bayliss.

He emerged from hospital, facing at least six weeks on crutches. She ascertained his home address and asked if she could visit him for a chat. He was a little over-awed to be visited by this rather 'posh bird', as he expressed it afterwards in his chauvinistic idiom, but after initial awkwardness, and cups of tea supplied by his mother, they got on quite well.

'You say this lady who caused your accident was young, in a fine blue dress, and was her hair in ringlets?' (She had to explain 'ringlets', but he caught on quickly. He may not have been very educated, but he wasn't stupid.)

'Yeh! That's exactly right.' he replied. Then Barbara produced the inventory book and opened it at the page displaying the coloured plate photograph of the portrait of Lady Sarah.

'Yes! Yes!', Terry cried excitedly. 'That's her! Bit of all right, isn't, she?'

Barbara felt tempted to agree, but wouldn't have quite put it that way. She had heard of Terry's original account to the police.

'"Great tits" was your description, I believe.'

Terry was a little embarrassed.

'But what was she doing jumping out in front of my van like that?', he asked.

'Quite remarkable, Terry', replied Barbara, 'considering she died in 1774. Sorry, you'll have to find someone else to ogle. And while we're on the topic', she said teasingly thrusting her bosom forwards, 'I'm not for sale.'

She had to chuckle at poor Terry. But there was not much else to laugh at.

So the mystery remained. It seemed as if Lady Sarah, having had her image destroyed, was determined to take her spinet with her into the void. Barbara was resolved, however, that Sarah would not disappear forever. She had a full length reproduction of the portrait produced and had Barton & Hayward build a replica of the spinet. These two items were duly installed in the Lodge.

On the night after, Barbara had a strange if rather gratifying dream. She was in the main drawing room which was lit by candlelight. There in front of her was a young woman, Lady Sarah, seated at her spinet playing a gigue. She finished playing, turned round and smiled, and Barbara woke.

She had saved Sarah for posterity. She could not ask for more.

Liam's imaginary friend

Many children have imaginary friends. Liam's father remembers having one called 'Weeman', not on account of his size, but because he was the fall guy who got the blame for the episodes of nocturnal enuresis which caused his parents some irritation until it gradually ceased by the age of nine. But Weeman survived the bed-wetting period, and apparently went on to have other adventures for a year or so.

So Liam's parents Ron and Fiona Webbe were not surprised to discover that he too had acquired a companion, although he had come on the scene quite late, since Liam was nearly ten. Fiona asked about the 'friend' who had a moniker which sounded like 'Playfool', which suggested he might be a potential source of mischief. The 'friends' of some children had a tendency to be a little impish. But 'Mr. Playfool' was to turn out to be interestingly different.

One day, Liam's sister Danielle heard Liam in his room. He seemed to be talking to somebody. She quietly peeked round the door to find Liam dancing around the middle of the floor. She was reluctant to disturb her brother, and retreated quietly.

'It's strange, Mum', she said to Fiona downstairs. 'Liam's up there dancing round his room as if he's with someone else. But there isn't anyone. You don't think he's gone loopy, do you?'

Fiona laughed. She tried to reassure Danielle that Liam was just indulging his imagination. Danielle didn't remember having any imaginary friends when she was younger, although she'd had vivid enough dreams from time to time. One evening, Ron and Fiona thought they might gently interrogate Liam further about 'Mr Playfool'.

'What's with the dancing, Liam?', Ron asked after their evening meal.

'Oh, Mr. Playfool teaches dancing. He's got some young girls with him. They help me with the steps.' Liam replied, as though there was nothing remotely remarkable about what he was saying.

Ron looked at Fiona. Was this an early sign of adolescence – fantasising about young girls (plural!)? They actually found it a little amusing.

Danielle still thought Liam was a bit odd, but avoided saying anything. Fiona continued to be curious. What an imagination Liam had – maybe he might develop into a writer. Some older pupils at his school did creative writing classes, and he might do the same next year. She then asked what Mr Playfool looked like.

'Oh, he's got funny clothes.'

Fiona stared.

'Funny clothes? You mean like a clown or something?'

Liam shook his head.

'No, he's got funny trouser things that stop round his knees, and shoes with buckles on. And he's got a frilly shirt and a wig thing.'

Fiona wondered what he meant by 'a wig thing'.

'Like those people wear in the cop shows – trials in court – only he's nothing to do with the law.'

And as for the girls? Liam described them as having long dresses and were very pretty and…. then he looked a little embarrassed and said something which suggested they were displaying a lot of cleavage! This was some fantasy. Ron joked that if it made him a great dancer, he might become a new 'Billy Elliot'.

Where did Liam get all this from? He wasn't given to spending every free hour on the computer or smart phone, although he used Google a lot. Perhaps he had unconsciously assimilated something he'd come across. He was, after all, musical like his sister.

When Fiona inquired further, she found that, according to Liam, Mr. Playfool taught dances playing an instrument.

'What sort of instrument does he play, Liam?' she asked.

'Well, it's sort of like Daniella's violin, only smaller – perhaps half the size, I don't know.', he replied.

Ron and Fiona found this a little puzzling. Surely a dancing teacher wouldn't be playing what, from Liam's description seemed to be an instrument more suitable for a child than an adult. And what were they to make of the costumes of Mr. Playful and the girls?

'Sounds like something from the 17th or 18th century.', Fiona speculated. Perhaps some research was called for.

As it happens, it was Daniella who was to make a sort of 'breakthrough'. Liam had no idea that his own little world had aroused such curiosity and interest.

Daniella's music teacher at school had a room filled with musical scores. But there were also quite a number of books, some of them works about musical history. One day, while she was in his room waiting for her weekly lesson, she occupied herself scanning the shelves. By chance she found an interesting item right at the end of the last shelf: 'The Dancing Master' by someone called John Playford (1623 -87), for solo violin. She asked her teacher if she could borrow it for a few days. He was a little surprised, but was happy to indulge her curiosity and have a go at playing the pieces.

She waited for a day when everyone else was out and engaged in some sustained practice. Was this the music that Liam had heard being played by his 'Mr. Playfool' (whom Danielle now suspected was in fact John Playford.)? She thought she would wait a day or two, and then when she felt confident, she would get everybody together and reveal her discovery.

So one Saturday after lunch, Danielle got her 'audience ', Liam and their parents seated in the lounge. She started playing the pieces from the book she had borrowed. Liam stood bolt upright.

'That's the music Mr Playfool plays when he's teaching me and the girls' he exclaimed.

'I think your Mr. Playfool is in fact John Playford, the man who produced this music. He lived in the seventeenth century, Liam. That explains the costume, his small teacher's violin - the whole thing. But how he has managed to enter your life in this way, search me!'

Liam's 'Mr Playfool' (aka Playford) gradually faded away. But Liam did become a dancer.

Losing Laura

One day Laura Payne left home and never returned. The children had seen her drive off in the red Ford Fiesta that she used as the 'run-about' for local trips, including those to the local arts centre where the Brentshire Philharmonic had their rehearsals.

She had for some years been leader and first violin, and was highly respected by the members and the conductor, Daniel Komisarczuk. Her husband Dominic was a solicitor and partner in the firm Wilson, Payne and Mortlake. Their three children, Simeon, Ruth and Maxine were 12, 10 and 8 years old at the time of their mother's disappearance, and their father was very badly affected and this manifested itself in his behaviour.

Laura's car had been found abandoned in a lay-by on the Clayton Castle Road, not far from the turn-off for the Meres, a well-known beauty spot popular with both locals and tourists in the summer months. Dominic had developed the habit of going out in his BMW, driving around the area visiting all the places which were associated with Laura both before and after they were married. This included the Meres.

The children were familiar with these lakes. Some people used to swim in them, although the general advice recommended against it. These desperate trips continued for several months, sometimes as often as three times a week, gradually diminishing over time until finally they ceased to take place except on the anniversary of her disappearance. Simeon felt he had to protect his siblings from themselves being disturbed by their father's behaviour, which, one supposes, was a form of grieving without the benefit of a grave to visit or an urn with ashes.

Naturally, in the early stages of their investigation, the police subjected Dominic to close questioning. He was sometimes less than coherent in his responses, but they could find no solid evidence to sustain their initial suspicion that he might have been responsible for his wife's disappearance. The children were also interviewed, but confirmed their memory of her departure. They were under the impression she was going to some meeting to do with the orchestra, but could supply no further details. They did not seem to be behaving as if they had been 'coached' in their replies by their father.

The police had asked Dominic some probing personal questions, trying to ascertain whether there were any domestic problems, affairs or other issues that might have prompted her to leave. But the fact was that she had left with just her handbag, car and house keys and a notebook. Apart from the clothes she had worn that day, nothing was missing from her wardrobe, dressing table drawers, or bathroom cabinet. Her violin remained on a table next to the baby grand piano in the lounge. None of her belongings were found in the abandoned car. It was as if she had been 'erased' from the world of her husband and children, and the orchestra to which she had belonged for more than ten years.

Ten years later, Simeon had left home and started his own decorating business with a workplace in one of the units on the local trading estate. He had acquired a flat in town which he shared with his partner Connie who worked for a local estate agent. Ruth was away from home in her second year at university, studying French and German.

Maxine remained at home. She was now in the sixth form studying music, literature and art. Of the three children, she had seemed to inherit her mother's musical talent and already had her Grade 8 in violin. She was hoping to study for a degree in music. But so marked was her ability that she was actually invited to join the Brentshire Philharmonic by Daniel Komisarczuk. She was warmly welcomed. The orchestra had been deeply upset by the loss of Laura, and it was almost as if they were having her restored to them in the form of her daughter. At home she would often play pieces that her mother used to play. Sometimes, Dominic found this difficult, and on one occasion rushed out of the house into the garden, looking tearful and distracted. But sometimes he responded with pleasure, as if consoled by the music.

The three siblings thought it would be a nice idea to get together and go somewhere they remembered enjoying as children – even having a picnic. They thought of inviting their father, but he declined. Simeon came with Connie and Ruth came home from university for the weekend. It was a beautiful sunny afternoon as they all made their way to the Meres, parked themselves on a grassy mound close to the water. Simeon had borrowed his father's car and they thought they might go for a drive afterwards.

In the event, Simeon, Connie and Ruth drifted off into a pleasant doze. Maxine, however, remained wide awake. It was quite still. Just a short distance away there were two men fishing, with a windbreak behind them, a little gas stove, and a basket. She smiled and waved at them. A little later, she heard a sound. It was a violin playing. She recognised the piece as one of her mother's favourites, Elgar's 'Salut d'Amour'. Where was the sound coming from? Not from the men fishing nearby – there was no sign of a radio. It almost seemed as if it were coming from somewhere below the bank. But it couldn't really be coming from there, surely. What surprised her was the fact that none of the others stirred, and when they eventually woke, they said that they hadn't heard anything at all.

By then the music had faded away, but for Ruth the memory lingered and almost troubled her. Was she imagining things? Had she actually nodded off herself and dreamt the whole thing? Simeon suggested that they go off to Clayton Castle. There was a good view of the county from there and they could take some photos as part of their 'nostalgia' trip.

The anniversary date approached and Maxine was bracing herself in anticipation of Dominic's mood. He was always less communicative than usual before setting off on this ritual outing. But there it was – she was hardly unused to this, but it never seemed to get any easier. Dominic had brief relationships with other women, but they had never really developed because Laura was 'still there'. So he said goodbye to Maxine and drove off.

After driving round several 'haunts', he took the turn off for the Meres, and was approaching the picnic spot his children had picked, when he started to hear violin music coming from the water. He then sustained a massive stroke and his car hurtled out of control into the Meres. The vehicle ended up in nearly 15 feet of water. Police divers finally managed to retrieve the car and Dominic's body was removed to the hospital mortuary.

But that was not all they found. Just a few feet away from the submerged car, they had located a large bundle wrapped in a tarpaulin and tied with thick cord. When opened up, a decomposed body was found with a ligature round the neck. Dental records established that the remains were those of Laura Payne, and that the body had been in that location for at least ten years.

What was puzzling was that there was no trace of Laura's wedding ring or bracelet. What had happened to them?

The police interviewed the children again. Once again they drew a blank. According to Simeon, his father had not left the house after returning home from work on the day of Laura's disappearance, and had been seen at work for several hours after Laura had left the house. The mystery remained.

The siblings had a harrowing time, having to arrange two funerals, but ones which could not be held at the same time. With the police and coroner involved, the process was drawn out and agonising.

Some months later, Maxine felt able to return to the Brentshire Philharmonic. She was welcomed back by everybody – well, almost everybody. One person was missing. One of the cellists, Patrick Freeman, had been absent from rehearsals since the time of her father's death and the discovery of her mother's body in the Meres. One of her other colleagues, Emma Lepore, a clarinettist, said that he had made several advances to her mother and had been firmly rebuffed. So there was no question of Laura having had an affair. Why was he absent? Could he not face the thought of seeing the daughter of the woman who had rejected him? There was one more shock to come.

A few days after she had re-joined the orchestra, the news broke that Patrick Freeman had been found dead at home. He had committed suicide. In a small bag found at the back of a desk drawer police found the wedding ring and bracelet belonging to Laura Payne.

Maxine's horror was mitigated by the fact that her father was no longer even posthumously under suspicion.

Musica de profundis

Werner Kessel was quite a character as well as being a renowned clarinettist. He had played with some of the leading orchestras, was the author of several books and had been responsible for instituting a bursary system for aspiring young musicians. He revealed the puckish side of his nature in various ways. He liked playing magic tricks, and a short book on magic was one of his 'non-professional' publications.

One of his more subversive jokes was at the expense of a conductor who was both a humourless martinet and disliked by the orchestra Werner played for. His trick in rehearsals was to wait until the players had started a piece or a movement and then play a deliberately discordant note randomly or irregularly. The said conductor would bring the playing to a halt and ask where the sound was coming from. Everyone would look blank, as if they had heard nothing. The players would start again and again the alien note would sound. This went on for some time, until the conductor stormed out uttering oaths. He left shortly afterwards, to be replaced by a more popular maestro with a sense of humour.

Kessel retired after nearly forty years with the city orchestra. He had planned to do one more concert tour and some recordings for leading labels like Deutsche Gramaphon. Sadly, it was not to be. Just six months into his retirement, he collapsed with a stroke and died three days later. His wife Helga was devastated as were his son and daughter (each themselves aspiring musicians who owed their father much of their inspiration).

The funeral was a grand affair, with many members of the orchestra present along with representatives of the many professional organisations with which he had been associated over the years. Werner was buried in the family vault, an impressive rather gothic-looking construction which had been built for his great grandparents who, for political reasons, had left Bismarck's Germany and settled in London. The vault had a sequence of shelves around the walls containing the coffins of those grandparents and other ancestors. Werner was placed on a specially newly made shelf directly opposite the entrance (which was six steps below ground level.)

In his will, Werner had made some stipulations in relation to the funeral. One was the request that he be buried with his beloved clarinet. His daughter was slightly disappointed, as she had hoped he might pass it to her. He had, however, been of the view that the player's relationship to an instrument is so personal and intimate. (Just as well he hadn't been a concert pianist. Wanting to be buried with a Steinway might have proved problematic!) Someone observed that he was behaving like a pharaoh, taking with him items for the afterlife

The orchestra leader suggested to Helga that they might hold a memorial concert featuring some of Werner's own favourite works. The provisional programme included works by Beethoven, Brahms, and Mozart. (The Mozart item was to be the clarinet concerto in A, K622, one of Werner's favourites which he had recorded more than once.)

Three months later, the concert was held in London, conducted by one of Werner's old friends, Heinrich Fischer. The concert was well attended, and Helga and her children received a round of applause as they entered the auditorium. The orchestra opened with the Beethoven 'Coriolan' overture.

It was then that something peculiar happened. Everyone in the orchestra and Fischer himself detected a discordant sound coming as if from the woodwind section. It was happening at random intervals throughout the piece. Rather than bring the performance to a halt, Fischer gallantly soldiered on. He recalled afterwards that it was nowhere near as bad as the time he had to play through the sound of a car alarm in the street outside one venue some years earlier.

So they reached the end, they and Beethoven surviving the interference. The Mozart proceeded without a hitch, being played by a young up and coming player, Anna Sechter. She received rapturous applause and a bouquet which almost dwarfed her diminutive figure.

Some of the money raised by the concert was put to supporting some of Werner's own projects. Someone put forward the idea that there might be a special competition for young musicians named after him, to be staged each year.

The family spent some time sorting through Werner's effects. Though by nature organised and meticulous in professional matters, he could be whimsical in the way he stored or shelved items. Perhaps that was his way of anticipating the fun his family might have searching for things in less than obvious places. Some of his music scores could be offered to the orchestra. An old and inferior clarinet might be found a home somewhere. And then there was something they had never seen before – a photograph of his great grandparents from about 1880. The grandfather was sitting in a luxurious armchair holding a clarinet. Helga had never known that there was music further back in the family, though it was not altogether a surprise.

Several weeks later, someone reported that, as they were passing the cemetery one night, they heard the sound of a clarinet playing – they guessed it was a clarinet because it reminded them of Acker Bilk's 'Stranger on the Shore'. As for the music itself, they had no idea what it was, except that it sounded like 'classical stuff'.

As time passed, there were more and more reports from people hearing a clarinet being played 'from somewhere inside the graveyard'. By chance one witness was a friend of an orchestra member and immediately identified the piece they heard as the slow movement from the Mozart concerto.

All this was reported to Helga and the rest of the family. How were they to respond to this extraordinary state of affairs? Was someone indulging in a cruel joke, perhaps playing a recording as people were passing? Why would they do that? And how would they get access to the place after dark. The gates were locked at 5.30, And there was a very high wall and railings round the cemetery. You would have to be pretty determined to try and scale walls for the sake of musical mischief.

Helga and the family decided to investigate for themselves and see if they might have similar experiences. One night they all assembled with cemetery staff who had been willing to collaborate in this odd nocturnal adventure.

'Council wouldn't approve of this.' said one.

Then, after a few minutes, while they were standing before the family vault, the music started – the slow movement from the Mozart concerto. When the movement concluded, the family decided to open the vault. They descended the steps and produced a variety of strong torches. They moved slowly into the vault. Their lights hovered over the dark degraded wooden homes of the long-dead, and then converged on Werner's own coffin which had what amounted to an almost privileged position directly in front of them. The braced themselves for their next action: to open the coffin. What were they expecting to find? Werner lying mischievously playing away in the dark? They unscrewed the lid, slowly sliding it to one side. Then they heard what sounded like someone chuckling.

The coffin was empty.

Santa's organ sleigh

Christmas Day morning service was traditionally the family service at St. Mary's, Flaxton Moor. The Rev. Sonya Webbe was anticipating a good turn-out, since she knew that more of the congregation had visiting relatives and friends this year. It was scheduled to be a short service, starting at 10.00 a.m. and ending at approximately 10.45. The Nine Lessons and Carols service had been held two days previously, so she didn't want a feeble repetition. A few hymns, a couple of readings, a brief address and an offertory for a homeless charity.

Jonathan Hayes, the organist, arrived early, intending to provide some pre-service music. However, on his way up to the organ, he tripped and twisted his ankle. He was in some discomfort, but said, stoically, that he would try and manage without the pedals. However, he was destined to be frustrated even in this. He switched on the blower, but there was a scraping sound and what seemed like a minor explosion. At which point the blower ceased to function. The instrument was mute. Jonathan and Sonya had a rather desperate conference in the corridor below the stairs. Unfortunately, the church piano had recently been removed to be refurbished and generally overhauled after years of neglect, and Jonathan was adamant that a keyboard would not be suitable or indeed adequate in such a large space. But what was to be done? You could hardly expect 80-100 people (including children) to attempt even the most familiar of seasonal hymns 'a capella'

People were puzzled why the start of the service had been delayed, although most of them had heard the noise from the blower. The younger children were starting to become restive, and Jonathan was wondering whether they would have to resort to what he called 'that bloody awful karaoke machine', with CDs of pre-recorded hymns. Sonya couldn't remember where it was stored anyway, and they didn't feel they could delay things much longer.

While everyone was speculating what was going to happen, one mischievous child started to sing 'Jingle Bells'. An embarrassed mother tried to silence him, but without success. But something else was about to silence him and everybody else.

Suddenly, there was a loud rushing noise and what sounded like little bells ringing. Through the West window there materialised an amazing sight – an enormous sleigh pulled by six pairs of reindeer with...Santa Claus seated behind pulling on the reins and shouting

'Whoa!'

The sleigh and its antlered cohort came to a halt, floating by some mysterious levitation nearly twenty feet above the congregation which occupied the front ten pews.

'Hello everyone!' Santa boomed. 'I believe you have a problem. Just finished my present deliveries. Speed of light, you know.'

No-one was disposed to argue with him; they were most of them gobsmacked.

'I'm going to help you'.

At this point, he gestured toward the rear of his sleigh. People craned their necks and looked up. There, positioned at the back of the sleigh, was a two manual organ (and pedals too, though they were not visible from below.) He called down to Sonya.

'Just tell me which hymns you want'.

He then said he would play a little pre-service music – improvisations on 'Silent night', a berceuse by Vierne as a meditation piece, and play everyone out to Bach's' Wachet Auf'. And No, he wasn't going to play 'White Christmas' from 'Holiday Inn'! Sonya asked if he would play something during the offertory. He said he had a lively little flute piece by Thorley which might 'cheer people up while they were parting with their money'. At this point he let rip with a loud guffaw.

He was about to start when he overheard two members of the congregation wondering how the instrument was powered. He leant over and boomed

'Angel wind!'

(What on earth was this? Some form of celestial flatulence? Sonja thought it better not to enquire. She thought that that might be crazy enough to work, whatever it was!)

Santa began the service with 'Adeste Fideles', followed by some of the other 'standards' and ending with 'Hark the herald...' Santa's instrument was effective and certainly powerful enough and the congregation responded enthusiastically. Jonathan and Sonya were relieved that their 'larger than life' visitor had saved the day. As Santa played 'Wachet Auf', everyone slowly filed out into the winter sunshine.

Then, the music ended, Santa swung the sleigh round, and he, sleigh and his team of reindeer, raced away down the nave and 'de-materialised' through the West window and vanished into the sunlight.

It was then that people noticed that they had all been showered with a fine silvery dust. They looked up into the sky and saw what looked like a vapour trail spelling out 'Merry Christmas!'

Terry's church in miniature

Terry Nares was invalided out of the army during a tour of duty in Afghanistan. He lost both legs below the knee as a result of a Taliban IED all but destroying the thinly armoured vehicle in which he was riding with several colleagues. Only he and one other actually survived the blast, largely because they were flung from the vehicle. After months of rehabilitation, Terry was having to think of his future, both in terms of jobs and recreation.

He had ideas of being a para-athlete. Before his army service, he had had an interest in archery, and with both his arms intact, pursuing this as a sport remained a perfectly reasonable possibility.

He also had an interest in modelling, not in the catwalk sense, but in the production of miniatures. As a child, he had been fascinated by model railways and had even made some model buildings for his layout. Now, as he was exploring the possibilities still open to him, the thought occurred to him that he would like to be a little more ambitious and produce something on a larger scale. Once, he Had visited St. Paul's in London, and he remembered seeing a large wooden model of the building in the crypt. As a child, he had attended St. Anselm's near his home, and now he thought it would be interesting to build a model of it which could be presented to the church whose present priest, Father Gerald Farnaby, had given him considerable support since he left the army, as had some members of the congregation.

He found church buildings awe-inspiring, and had always been stimulated by the music – especially the exit voluntaries performed by the organist. He had an idea to fashion his model, not in wood, but in carefully crafted miniaturised stone, albeit mounted on a wooden frame. With his partner Jill, he turned the garage into a workshop, and acquired lathes, saws and all manner of equipment.

The church supplied him with a brochure containing a diagram – a ground-plan in effect, of the building, and Father Gerald was very generous with his time, supplying information of various kinds. He had a friend in the building trade who was able to supply him with bits of discarded concrete and sandstone, as well as off-cuts of timber. With this all assembled, Terry was able to start the project of planning and construction. He was quite adept with computer graphics and quickly produced 3D images of the church using the materials to hand.

It was nearly a year later before Terry's project was close to completion. With skilful wiring, the interior of the model church could be illuminated, and all its features revealed. He had achieved a remarkable feat, capturing the detail of St. Anselm's. He had had fun constructing the miniature version of the organ.

The organist, Frederick Chipp, had given him a lot of useful hints. Terry thought it would be fun to make a model through which recordings of organ music could be played – using small speakers at the rear of the model building. A friend, who was a skilled electrician, helped out with this subtle task.

Finally, Terry arranged to have the model transported to the church, where it was to be installed in the newly built glass-fronted entrance lobby. There was to be a ceremony, with various guests, including the mayor and senior clergy. Terry had made part of the roof of his model into a lid that could be lifted so that people could see inside. Fred Chipp gave a short recital after the ceremony, crowning a very fulfilling day for Terry and Jill. But the story does not end there.

Some weeks later, a fault developed in the electrical circuitry, with the consequence that the music could not be played through the speakers at the back of the model. Despite his best efforts and those of the electrician, the source of the fault could not be located. Terry was not looking forward to having to dismantle part of his model to try and trace the problem. For the moment at least, they decided to leave things as they were.

Which is how they stayed until one evening a month later. Father Gerald was over at the church, working in the vestry, part of which also functioned as an office. He heard sounds coming from somewhere in the church.

'Organ music?' he thought.

But Fred wasn't in the church, and besides, the sound wasn't really loud enough for it to be him playing. Father Gerald went through to the church and followed the sound all the way to the lobby. He couldn't believe what he saw – and heard. There was Terry's model, fully illuminated, and the sound of organ music coming from inside. But that was not all.

He lifted the roof lid and beheld the most amazing sight. The inside of the church was full of tiny people sitting on little chairs. And most disconcertingly of all, there at the front before the altar, was a tiny version of himself, and above the West door was a miniature Fred Chipp playing the organ!

More remarkably, in the lobby of the model, Father Gerald could see what was clearly a model of the church! He could not remember Terry incorporating such a thing into the model, but he became rather dizzy at the thought that this too might contain an even smaller version of St. Anselm's and so on ad infinitum!

Not altogether surprisingly, as a result of this contemplation of potentially limitless replication, Father Gerald passed out, and was found by one of his juniors the following morning, fast asleep on the floor. When he awoke he had no memory of what he had experienced the previous evening. But miraculously, the model church seemed to have put itself back in working order by the time Terry revisited the church later in the week. He was never to know that his model had acquired a life of its own.

The busker

Wenthorpe Abbey is, over and above its ecclesiastical status, something of a visitor attraction. Situated on the town square, it is also the location for the chalets of the Christmas market. These are usually installed along the railings on the North side of the building.

For most of the year however, the paving alongside these railings is occupied by various 'entertainers'. Some are more transient visitors – 'artistes' associated with festivals, but others are locals. You get people who sing (or suffer from the delusion that they can), drummers, jugglers, and various eccentrics peddling esoteric items that induce frowns among the clergy.

The biggest complaint comes from the abbey organist Jonathan Webbe, who gets irritated by the cacophony outside while endeavouring to play a quiet interlude during the weekday communion services. He is especially proud of the new Klais organ recently installed as a replacement for the defunct Harrison. It sits proudly on the balcony with its fine light wood casework complementing the gothic architecture.

The Abbey escaped the worst of Henry VIII's vandalism, but had been subject to various phases of restoration, the most recent being carried out in the 19th century. There had originally been a wooden roof on the nave, but this had caught fire and was replaced with rib-vaulting tastefully done in keeping with the mediaeval character of the Abbey. The graceful lines of the building are a little spoiled by the large number of plaques on the walls commemorating the great and, in some cases, the not so good.

Outside the Abbey, there was a well-known character who was regularly seen on his own 'pitch' by the railings, close to the Abbey notice board. In appearance he looked rather like a tramp or vagrant. In winter, he would wear a shabby trench coat, but regardless of weather or season, he would always wear a rather discoloured bowler hat. At his feet was an old blue battered violin case which lay open for contributions from the passing public. He was such an attraction that he did rather well out of a large quantity of small change. He was extremely versatile. He could play folk tunes and dances, but also pieces from the classical repertoire from Bach to Brahms, and he could bring tears to people's eyes with his rendition of the Meditation from Thaïs by Massenet. He could also entertain on the flute. Occasionally, he would play pieces on request, and he was adept at improvisation. He would certainly have intrigued Jonathan Webbe, although it would have been hard to imagine them in concert together, the one dapper in smart suit, the other threadbare and unkempt.

Just now and then, the lane by the railings is cleared for special events, particularly ceremonies and major services in the Abbey. One month, there were several such occasions, and the entertainers were moved on. Some of them found alternative locations elsewhere in the town centre, but our lone virtuoso apparently did not. At least no-one saw him after the first 'clearing' of the lane. It was assumed that he had given up and moved elsewhere.

Several months passed and there was no sign of him. He was missed, and for a while no-one presumed to take his space by the railings. Eventually, a group of young musicians from the local music college claimed the spot. They were a quartet of string players, and had heard stories about the absent eccentric they had replaced in the lane. They earned a measure of approval when they demonstrated their own versatility playing some of the pieces he used to play. Mercifully, they did not have to contend with inept, tone-deaf 'singers'. These seem to have moved on to inflict torment on listeners in some other location. For a while, the entertainers in the Abbey lane were undisturbed. However, a notice posted on the notice-board gave advance notification of a large funeral that was to be held at the Abbey in a few days' time. Everyone moved out of the lane and traffic cones were positioned along the entire North side of the building.

Come the day, a large crowd had assembled near the Abbey. The police had roped off the area immediately in front of the West front of the building. Just before the West door stood eight young soldiers in uniform, positioned in line. These were to be the coffin bearers. They had already been standing patiently for some time, and although the funeral was scheduled to start at 11.00 a.m., things seemed to be running a little behind schedule. This wasn't surprising, given that the centre of town was a bit of a bottle-neck, a problem partly due to increased pedestrianisation. The crowd grew. One person asked a WPC whose funeral it was.

'It's for Captain Sir Leighton Hewitt Stanton. He was an industrialist and patron and benefactor of the Abbey, I believe.', she replied. It further emerged that Sir Leighton had served in the Falklands campaign and one tour of duty in Afghanistan.

A few minutes later, the hearse and two funeral cars approached up the lane. Some senior clergy, appeared on the steps of the West door. The bearer party took up their position at the rear of the hearse. Family emerged from the funeral cars and stood and waited while the coffin was lifted from the hearse and shouldered ready to proceed into the Abbey. The crowd, which had been restive and a little noisy, now fell into a reverential silence. A bell tolled. There followed a brief period of silence and anticipation. And then from within the abbey, one could hear the organ. Jonathan Webbe was playing an organ transcription of the Meditation from Thaïs. The bearer party started to move towards the door, with the family cortege following in line behind them. On the coffin, resting amidst a large spray of lilies, was an old blue violin case and a shabby bowler hat.

The cats' quartet

'Paws' was the family cat. But Paws was very much Jenny's cat. She had arrived when Jenny was just three.

Now Jenny was nearly 14, and the hormones were making her more maverick and irritable. Other humans had become alien, especially adults. 'Just a phase' was the cliché response to the phenomenon.

But 'just a phase' was not helped by something that occasioned her considerable grief. Paws died. She died in her basket in the kitchen. She had not been well for a while. The vet had suspected a malignancy and her kidneys had started to fail. In a way, her dying like this seemed more 'natural' than having to take her to the vet's to be 'put to sleep'. (Jenny hated this phrase. It seemed so false. It wasn't as if an animal would somehow wake up afterwards, was it?).

For a while afterwards, Jenny was off her food, moodier than before, and her performance at school had become erratic. 'Just a phase' looked like lasting some time.

Jenny's Mum Lynne had a sister Caroline. Jenny's birthday was immanent, and Caroline was wondering what present to get for her. Then she had an idea. There was a shop in the High Street which sold all manner of ornaments and bric-a-brac. But what caught her eye among the window displays was a set of four china figures – cats, each playing a musical instrument. One had a violin, another a cello, one a viola and the one at the back a piano. As Jenny was musical and currently studying for her Grade 5 piano, Caroline thought it would be the ideal present.

It worked. Come the day, Jenny was delighted, and was actually smiling for the first time in weeks. The cats were given pride of place on her bedside table next to the clock. They were the first things she saw when she woke up. She fancifully christened them 'The Paws Quartet'. She was sure Paws would have approved.

Jenny had a photo album. One of her favourite items was a picture of Paws which she removed and put in her bedside drawer. She had many photos of Paws, of course, but she considered it was the best out of her collection. She even bought a special frame for it.

She started to 'lighten up'. She still missed Paws, but was 'moving on', as they say. In a way, the cat quartet had had a therapeutic effect. It was about to have rather more than that.

One Saturday morning, Jenny was in her room and had taken the picture of Paws out of the drawer. It was then that she heard the music. She looked up. There were her four cats playing their instruments, rocking to and fro in time to the music. Jenny recognised some of the music they played. She owned some piano solo versions of the pieces which she used for practice for her grade exams. How long were they going to play for? She put the photo back in the drawer and got up from her bed. The music stopped immediately. The cats became quite still.

And so it was that Jenny came to notice that it was only when she took Paws' photo out of the drawer that the cats would play. And if either of her parents came into the room, the music would stop instantly. They would play only for Jenny, in memory of Paws.

The harmonious poltergeist

Our house is what you call a 'new-build', one of the larger kind with three stories, and the lounge on the second floor. There is what one might hesitate to call a lawn in front. (The initial lumpiness we found was due to an old cement bag having been buried under the turf.) There's a larger garden to the rear, with possibilities of development. The estate is fairly recent. Certainly nothing to lead you to expect anything particularly bizarre or 'spooky' of the type you might associate with older properties. And nothing untoward happened for the first two or three years.

Sam (Samantha) was our first child. Quiet, with a thoughtful temperament. Nothing much to disturb our nights after the first three months. Pip (Philip) arrived two years later. Again, nothing unusual for the first few years. Then, when he was about 5, he started to have disturbed nights, nightmares, episodes of sleepwalking, calling out, saying things we found unintelligible. He appeared to have no recollection of these events in the morning.

Pip settled down well in primary school, and teachers began to notice early signs of musical talent. (Sam had exhibited talents in art and drawing.) So it was that he commenced having piano lessons. We already owned a baby grand piano which occupied one corner of the lounge. My wife Maureen herself taught music at the local secondary school, and she was proud of her 'Pleyel' instrument. The company was no longer manufacturing pianos, so hers was one of the last to be produced. She was concerned to look after it and have it well maintained. Pip was to have the advantage of learning on a quality instrument. He took to it well, and seemed to have a 'feel' for it. No danger of crude thumping and plonking from him!

Then it started. After a few months, Pip became a little withdrawn, and there was a recurrence of nocturnal restlessness. That, however, was not all. One night, Maureen and I heard crashing and banging noises from downstairs. We both got up, half-expecting to find intruders in the process of burgling the house, but when we arrived in the lounge, we saw a number of items scattered around, two chairs and a coffee table upended, and the remnants of a porcelain vase spread around the fireside rug. We didn't shed any tears over the vase. It was frankly hideous, a 'gift'(?) from Maureen's sister-in-law whose taste was, as they say, 'in her mouth'. We had got used to it being on the mantelpiece behind some more aesthetic items which had amazingly remained in place. We left it till the morning to clear up, checked in Pip's room and found him fast asleep.

No more problems for a week or so, then another disrupted night. More crashing and banging following a sleep-walking episode from Pip. Another quick scamper down the stairs. More items scattered about, some books had been sent flying from the shelves. Then Maureen noticed that some of her music had been dislodged from the piano, though not scattered carelessly like the other items in the room. We tidied up, and sat over breakfast wondering what, if anything, we could do about this irritating phenomenon. We cautiously asked some neighbours whether they had heard or noticed anything. Some claimed that they had heard noises coming from our house in the small hours. When we described our experience to one of them, they facetiously observed that perhaps we should get the vicar of St. Dunstan's to 'exorcise' the house. Someone else ventured the hypothesis that some of these phenomena could be caused by underground streams or earth movements. I'd heard this latter kind of explanation before, but one could hardly remedy the problem by trying to divert an underground stream!

Pip became increasingly moody. Although this affected some of his schoolwork, it didn't interfere with his musical progress at all. His teacher remarked on his precocious talent. He was already attempting pieces beyond his estimated grade, and Maureen had to restrain his enthusiasm by pointing out the dangers of trying to run before you can walk. For a short while, things seemed to have calmed down, and we were all getting a decent night's sleep.

Remarkably, Sam had been the least affected. We always said that she could probably sleep through a volcanic eruption. Different people came to the house from time to time, but neither they nor we noticed anything untoward for quite a few weeks.

We wondered about staying up one night to see what happened. Sam thought we were mad. If someone (or something) were throwing things about, we might get injured. On the other hand, neighbours might grow impatient at these night-time disturbances. The police might be called and they might be a bit sceptical if we told them that the racket was caused by an invisible agent and not us! I'm not sure how we expected to stop a 'poltergeist' from indulging in these antics.

We'd even christened our intruder 'Poltie'. (We had no basis for attributing gender. Noisy ghosts could be male or female, presumably, though which ones were noisier – well that could lead to rather sexist jokes.) Well, whether 'she' or 'he', Poltie didn't keep us waiting long before performing again. ('perform') proved to be quite an apt description.)

Once again, it was the small hours. No crashes and banging this time. No sound of things being flung around or being broken. There was definite movement, but much more like the sound of someone moving quietly about the lounge. What were they up to? We weren't prepared for what happened next.

Suddenly, there was a violent sequence of chords being played on the piano. Maureen recognised it immediately. It was the opening of Beethoven's eighth piano sonata. What followed was a performance of the entire first movement. We sat up in bed riveted. Amazingly, Pip had remained in his room. Sam had rushed into our bedroom, half-awake, thinking that her mum had 'flipped' and started playing the piano in the middle of the night! No, this was Poltie giving us a dramatic surprise. But enjoyable though the music was, we could hardly endure this sort of thing at night, and the neighbours would really have something to complain about!

Absurd though it was, we thought of leaving a note on the piano overnight in future. We wrote: 'please, Poltie could you avoid playing loud music during the night. Thank you.' Believe it or not, it seemed to work.

No more disturbed nights, not even virtuoso musical performances. That, at last looked like the end of our problem. Not quite.

One morning, we all came down to breakfast as usual. As we were sitting in the kitchen, we heard the sound of the piano coming from the lounge. Once again, Maureen recognised the music. It was the last movement of Handel's Suite No.5 in E major, HWV 430 for harpsichord, with its five variations. Maureen told Pip that one day soon he might be able to play this well-known piece. We all listened to it right to the end. When we looked in the lounge, there was no-one there. But we had been well entertained. There was not a little irony in the fact that Maureen's maiden name was 'Black' and my own name was the rather common and boring 'Smith'.

Pip grew out of his 'phase' and continued to develop as a musician. After a while, 'Poltie' ceased to be active and we were no longer disturbed at night.

The harpist of Tŷ Pen Rhiw

'So where did you hear about Tŷ Pen Rhiw?' enquired the staff member at the Tourist information centre. The two visitors replied that they were interested in tracing their roots. The old house, built in around 1690 with subsequent additions in 1706, was associated with some of their ancestors, including the first owner, Sir Glyn Evans Davies. His grandson, Tomos Evans Davies, had emigrated in 1765.

'So you're from the other side of the 'pond', as they say' replied the guide.

'Yes, but we're actually Canadian – from Vancouver.', the two said, almost in chorus. (They didn't like people assuming they were 'yanks'.)

John and Kim Anderson were wondering if it might be possible to visit the house, as well as the small village church nearby which might contain some ancestral graves. The guide said that the property was not open to the general public, but he could ask the local council (the current owners) for permission for access. This had been granted on one or two previous occasions. The couple would probably have to be accompanied on any such visit, although they might have the freedom to wander about for themselves. They were hardly likely to run off with valuable paintings or silverware. They were told that a visit should be possible in a day or so.

'I'm Martin, by the way. I'll give you a call, and then you can come back here, and I'll give you a lift there, OK?'

Tŷ Pen Rhiw is a modest house, elegant, compact and very much of its time. Set in just a few acres, there are the remnants of what had been a small orchard at the rear. Extensive restoration work was being carried out with a view to making it into a tourist attraction, perhaps with a shop and café attached. Many of the art objects which had been in temporary storage would have to be returned and alarm systems installed. Staff would have to be hired, and provision made for a visitors' car park nearby. That was for the future.

What John and Kim saw when they arrived with Martin a week later resembled a building site. However, Martin stressed that much of the interior work was complete, and it was perfectly safe to walk around. He unlocked the front door, and they went inside.

'I'll stay in the car. Take as long as you like. I don't have to be back in the office today.'

With that, the couple strolled through the handsome entrance hall with its magnificent staircase.

'It actually seems larger than you might expect from the outside', Kim remarked.

They explored the rooms systematically. The first was the dining room, with a very large table concealed under a protective dust cover. Then there was what looked like the main downstairs drawing room. They discovered that the house had a basement which contained a large kitchen and what was probably a laundry room. Upstairs were several sizable bedrooms. The windows looked out over the fields to the north and the river to the south, with the main road to town running alongside. The last room to be viewed was downstairs near the entrance and opposite the dining room. This was obviously the library, with the walls lined with shelving. Many books were still present, but hidden under drapes which looked like old curtains that had seen better days. The only furniture in the room was a pair of matching and very stylish chairs and a small embroidered stool. They sat down for what they intended to be a brief rest before re-joining Martin outside.

They had been sitting for just a few minutes when they heard a sound, quite faint at first, but then growing louder. It was clearly the sound of a harp being played. Both John and Kim were music teachers, and listened intently to the music. They guessed that it was from the 18th century. One or two pieces sounded like they might be by Handel, others were probably old ballad tunes they could not immediately identify. They felt like staying longer, but they did not want to keep Martin waiting too long. As they got up to go, the music faded away.

Martin was standing beside his car puffing on a cigarette.

'Caught me!', he said with a slightly guilty smile. 'Must give it up. I've been trying to cut down for months.'

They set off back to town.

'We liked the music', the couple commented. 'When did you have the sound system installed?'

Martin looked in his rear-view mirror. He looked a little taken aback.

'Music? There's no sound system in the house for relaying music, although come to think of it, it would be a nice idea – give a period 'feel' to the place when it's finally opened', he replied.

John and Kim looked at each other. Could they have nodded off and dreamt the whole thing? Hardly. They earnestly repeated their claim to have heard music. Martin didn't reply directly, but changed the subject rather awkwardly. He delivered them back to their hotel.

They asked if they could make another trip out to visit the church to look at the graves of ancestors. Martin said he was likely to be busy for the next few days, but he had a friend who was a taxi driver who could take them out there as a special favour. The couple had the impression that Martin was being evasive on the music issue. Their intuition was right. This was not the first time he had had visitors to that house who had reported similar experiences.

Two days later, John and Kim were delivered to the little church, a small mediaeval building with a surprisingly large graveyard. They quickly found several tombstones bearing the names of people from the earlier Evans Davies period. As they were leaving, they stopped by the grave of a young woman who had died aged only 25. The stone was inscribed with the name 'Mair Siencyn' and the rest of the inscription was in Welsh. They hoped that someone might translate for them, so they copied the details as accurately as they could. They walked down the lane towards the house.

'Pity it's not open. Martin didn't seem as if he would be keen to let us in a second time. What's he hiding, John?', Kim asked.

John shrugged. He was just as puzzled as she was. They thought they'd look round the outside which they hadn't paid much attention to before. They entered the drive and saw two men working on a wall at the side of the house. Another man emerged from the house carrying some tools and a portable workbench.

'Mind if we go in and have a look?' they asked.

'Not sure about that.' came the reply.

They looked imploringly.

'OK Look, for God's sake don't tell anyone I let you in. I'll get a bollocking or even the sack. We're all knocking off for lunch now. Make sure and pull the door tight behind you when you leave. By the way, you sound American. Over here on holiday?'

They corrected him gently on nationality and thanked him for his indulgence.

So for a second time they seated themselves in the library. They heard the workmen switch off their radio and drive off. Everything was pleasantly still, except for the sound of birds in the trees and cows in the fields. Then they looked across the room to the corner containing the stool. A sort of strange mist filled that part of the room, and as they watched, they saw a figure emerging from the haze. In moments they found themselves looking at a pretty young woman in what they took to be traditional Welsh costume. (It was like pictures they'd seen in books about Wales.) Just as remarkable was the fact that she was seated on the stool with a large harp resting against her left shoulder. John stammered out the question

'Who are you?'

The woman hesitated. Perhaps his accent was the problem. Then she spoke:

'Mair ydw i. Mair Siencyn. Wyt ti'n hoffi fy ngherddoriaeth?'

John and Kim gasped.

'That must be Welsh', Kim said. 'I think the first bit was telling us that she's Mair Siencyn! John, she's a ghost!'

But somehow they didn't feel at all scared, just amazed. What they had not understood was that she had asked if they liked her music. She overcame the difficulty by pointing to her instrument. Then she started to play. They recognised some of the pieces from their first visit.

'Dafydd y Garreg Wen', she announced, and then in stumbling English, 'David...of...the White...Rock'. She accompanied herself singing several songs in a beautiful soprano voice, followed by several instrumental pieces which reminded them of some they had heard played on a harpsichord.

After nearly half an hour of performing for her 'guests' she rose and said:

'Diwedd. Diolch yn fawr iawn. Pob bendith.'

And then she disappeared, harp and all, leaving just the empty stool.

'Wasn't she lovely?', said Kim as they closed the door behind them. 'So sad she died so young. She was obviously a fine musician. It would be nice to find out more about her.'

They walked further down the lane to the main road. They would have the option of waiting for a bus or phoning Martin's friend for another lift. As they were walking along, they came close to the entrance to the nearby farm. The owner, Tudur Williams, was working close to the gate. Exchange of greetings.

'You've seen her then?' he asked.

The couple were taken aback at this. They had had two days of surprises.

'Oh, this happens from time to time', he continued. 'Other folk, visitors like you, have been here – heard the music and seen Mair. But she only appears and plays for 'sensitives' as my brother-in-law calls them. He's a psychologist at the university, by the way. Most people think he's crackers. But the point is that none of the visitors were suffering from disorders – you know – schizophrenia or whatever. Anyway, it's not being widely publicised. There's always a danger that real nutters and charlatans would descend on the place and end up being a bloody nuisance. And I don't want people buggering around my farm either.'

Then they mentioned Martin's evasiveness.

'Oh, Martin's my nephew. That's the point. He's being guarded about it for that very reason. Nothing against you. You're bona fide folk – over here tracing ancestors? Yes, that's what the other folks were doing. Some of them actually related to Mair. She was a music teacher and became a governess to the children of the owners of Tŷ Pen Rhiw after the Evans Davies family. I think their name was Parry, and I believe they were related to Parri Ddall or 'Blind Parry' the renowned harpist to the Watkins Wyn family. You can see his portrait by his son in the National Museum in Cardiff. Sadly, Mair died quite young, probably from TB, although they called it 'consumption' back then.'

The couple were impressed by Tudur's knowledge, but he pointed out that he was a bit of a fraud because his eldest daughter was a musician – in fact a harpist. She, unlike poor Mair, was in the best of health.

On their last night in the area, John and Kim retired early. There was a long journey ahead before their flight to Toronto. They had had an interesting, peculiar but satisfactory adventure. They were amazed that a long dead young woman had made such an impression on them. They both felt a kind of affection for her, which in a bizarre way was soon reciprocated. They both fell into a dream state, stirring after a short while to see a mist forming by the window of their room. Within a few seconds, there at the end of their bed, stood Mair Siencyn. She leant forward, blew them a kiss, and vanished into the night.

The music box

Well, I was told it was a music box. It was a box and a very handsome item too, walnut with fine inlay and brass fittings on the outside, and a smooth plush velvet lining within. On the underside was a key, presumably for winding up the mechanism – except there was no mechanism. There was a cavity below the velvet lined compartment, but it was empty. I never managed to get an explanation of this.

My aunt had owned it for as long as I could remember, but I never heard a sound from it over the years. I simply assumed it had stopped functioning on account of wear and tear or clogging up with dirt. That was what prompted me to investigate it, when I finally acquired it last year through her will.

I took it to one or two experts, who confirmed that it was, or had been a musical box, but were puzzled why it no longer contained any mechanism at all. One of them said that sometimes you would find a part of the mechanism missing, like the 'comb' – the set of steel 'prongs' that were 'pinged' by the spikes on a small rotating drum. These could become worn or broken, sounding off pitch or not at all. I got the impression that to replace the entire mechanism could be quite costly, unless I was lucky enough to find one salvaged from another box. So I resigned myself to retaining the box as an attractive wooden ornament taking its place along with some other items – boxes, turned plates and bowls, and even some figurines I had purchased at a fair.

My researches led me to conclude that the box was probably mid-nineteenth century and may itself have been part of a collection. But my aunt did not appear to own any other such items, and she never mentioned how she came by it. She always said that I could have it, since it had no sentimental value for her. I seem to recall that she kept spare change in it, since on one occasion after returning from the shops, she decanted a fistful of coins in it. I don't think she had any aesthetic appreciation of such things. (She managed to smash a valuable vase with rough handling!) So I suppose I was thankful that the box was intact, albeit minus the music component.

That, you might think, was the end of the matter. I gave no further thought to the box, other than on those occasions when visitors were invited to look in the display cabinet. The days and weeks passed without anything worthy of report.

Then, one afternoon when I was quietly reading in the lounge, I distinctly heard music coming from the display cabinet, the music of a musical box. I got up and went over to the cabinet and lifted out the box, and the sound immediately stopped. I was trying to identify the melody. I examined the box, even opening the base. It was empty as before. I replaced it in the cabinet, and lingered for a few minutes. But nothing further happened. So I went back to my chair and continued reading.

The hours passed, but no more sound came from the display cabinet, and I was beginning to wonder whether I was hallucinating or dreaming, although I don't think I nodded off at any point. Come 11.00 p.m., I turned in for the night. It was very quiet by contrast with the previous two nights when there had been howling gales and lashing rain. Nothing to disturb sleep this time. Or so I thought.

I stirred. I looked at the bedside clock. 3.45. I got up and shuffled across the landing to the toilet. The sound of the flush subsided and I heard musical sounds coming from downstairs. I went to the top of the stairs. I slowly crept down and started to recognise the music. It was Beethoven's well-known Bagatelle 'Für Elise'. What amazed me was that it seemed to be complete, not the truncated versions that you often get, especially with cheap 'commercial' boxes. I got to the cabinet and the music stopped. It was almost as if I was being teased by this object. Why?

From then on, the box played intermittently at different times of the day and night. I then came to a decision. Despite the expense, I would try and obtain a new mechanism for the box in the hope that I might be able to exert some control over it. I consulted a number of websites and went back to one of the experts I had dealt with before. He said he would try and get me a mechanism that would be suitable and would fit the box and winder.

Several weeks passed, and I had almost got used to the perversity of the box's behaviour. I found that if I closed the lounge door tight and my bedroom door, too, then I could hope for relatively undisturbed sleep. During the day, it mattered rather less, and the radio or T.V could be made loud enough to cover the brief bursts of sound from the cabinet. For a while, I had been unable to tell friends and neighbours in case they thought I was 'losing it'. Bur one day, George came round and his visit happened to coincide with a 'performance'. At first, he thought I was winding him up, or rather managing some remote winding of the box. But he knew from before that it had no mechanism. It was his turn to do some head scratching.

Eventually, my expert got back to me to say that he had managed to get hold of a suitable mechanism and would fit it for me if I took into his workshop. He was a bit busy, but said it should be ready in two days' time. Well that was two days' silence. Very much like the proverbial clock ticking – after a while, you only notice when it stops.

So, two days later, I collected the box. In my haste, I didn't play it in the workshop. I was just relieved to be taking it home in a complete condition. I would at last be able to control this mechanism. So I wound up the box. And there came the distinct sound of 'Für Elise', only this time it sounded only when I turned the key. It was almost as if the box had been seeking its missing music machine all along.

The old organ shoes

There is not much light in the wardrobe, although a little gets in through a narrow gap between the doors. On its floor sits a raked shoe rack. On the highest level sit a number of rather smart shoes belonging to Andrew and Elspeth Taylor. Immediately below are two pairs of sandals. On the very bottom are a pair of smart silver shoes and a pair of shabby-looking scuffed brown lace-ups. Andrew and Elspeth are both professional organists and these are their playing shoes. Andrew has had his shoes for years and they are like old friends. He's used to them, and finds them comfortable. No-one sees them when he's playing, so the incongruity between his smart concert suit and the footwear is rarely noticed. But the time is approaching for them to be replaced with purpose made lighter shoes of the sort regularly advertised in professional journals and magazines.

   Andrew's facetious name for his old shoes is 'Bill and Ben'. He's too young to remember a children's TV programme featuring flowerpot men mumbling unintelligibly to a large weed, but he recalls being told about it by his parents, and somehow the double name got itself adopted for various things down the years, including anything that came in pairs. However, they had resisted using the names for their children, not least because they were girls! So that brings us back to the wardrobe.

   Daughters Emily and Vicky were highly imaginative, and weren't above making up things – experiences, seeing witches in the garden, etc. So their parents were slightly underwhelmed when they were told by the girls that they often heard sounds coming from Mum and Dad's wardrobe. When asked, the girls said it sounded like mumbled talking. Andrew told Elspeth that what the girls were hearing and describing rather fancifully were noises in the domestic pipework.

'Sometimes happens if there's a temporary small airlock.' Andrew said. 'Usually clears when you flush the toilet.'

The girls were not convinced when given this explanation, because they heard the sound from time to time when there was no obvious 'rumblings' in the pipes and the flushing of the toilet didn't seem to make any difference at all. Perhaps the girls were not so wide of the mark.

Inside the wardrobe, there were various exchanges going on. The shoes on the topmost rack were making themselves particularly obnoxious and arrogant. They were the Taylors' best shoes for smart occasions and did they know it. They were especially rude to the sandals immediately below them. 'Poor things. So sparse and indecently casual. You've no right to be sharing space with us. Why aren't you downstairs in the conservatory with those dreadful flip-flop things and those vulgar gardening boots?', the three 'posh' pairs said in chorus. The sandals protested.

'You daren't walk anywhere for long – not in the rain, not on the beach, and at least the owners' feet don't get sweaty and horrible like they do wearing you to some of those fancy social 'dos'. That's why they fling you off as soon as they get home and put on the slippers in the hallway. But then you look down upon the slippers too, don't you? They're blest not being cooped up here with you six pretentious nobodies!'

The uppity six were fuming. Elspeth's silver organ shoes had been listening to this exchange. 'I don't know where you lot get your delusions from. We at least manage to be both smart and functional. When was the last time you were ever worn in performances of fine music?'

The six fumed even more, and thought they would get some compensation targeting the old shoes belonging to Andrew.

'You can't say you're smart can you? Well get this. We hear the owner is planning to replace you, so there!'

The old shoes replied. 'Look here, you twerps. We were being worn for years before you were even made. Yes, we started out being 'best' shoes for 'show', and we were a darn sight better made than any of you six, rest assured of that. When those days were past, we still had years of useful existence left, witness the fact that Mr Andrew has worn us for the past twenty years for playing. He obviously found us comfortable and more than adequate for the task. We wouldn't give you a chance of surviving that long or being that useful, come to that. So stop being so up yourselves. There are many worse things than having to share a shoe rack with the rest of us.'

The weeks passed. Andrew wore his old shoes as usual. Then a parcel arrived in the post. It was a shoe box containing a new pair of organ shoes. They were very slim-line (ideal for pedal work, reducing the risk of hitting more than one note) and black and shiny. Andrew tried them one and was very pleased. Later the wardrobe opened, and the new shoes were placed in the middle of the rack.

The old shoes looked at the newcomers suspiciously, the 'posh' ones with something amounting to hostility.

'Hello!', the new shoes said. 'We are the new organ shoes ordered by Mr. Taylor.'

The old shoes sighed.

'What's going to happen to us?' they cried.

The new shoes tried to be consoling.

'Oh. We were listening to Mr. Taylor. I think he said he was going to take you to the church and leave you by the organ there – for regular use on Sundays and so forth. So you will still be used for a while yet.'

The old shoes breathed a sigh of relief. This wasn't the end after all, and even if it meant a reduced role, it was better than being totally discarded after all these years of service. Besides, it would be bliss not to have to endure the 'snooty six' any more, even it was lonely up in the organ loft.

Even now, the arrogant six couldn't resist having a malicious 'dig' at the old shoes. 'I wouldn't bet on further use if we were you. I bet Taylor will get himself another pair of these light-weight 'things', and you will end up in the potting shed for gardening, if you're lucky.' The old shoes erupted.

'GARDENING! GARDENING?' At which point, the sandals said that they thought they heard someone coming up the stairs, so everyone had better be quiet.

'So why don't you shut up, then?' the arrogant six replied, mockingly and loudly saying 'SSH!'. The old shoes had the last word.

'You lot bloody SSH! yourselves.'

Emily and Vicky had just reached the top of the stairs. Emily turned to Vicky and said,

'Did you hear someone say 'SSH!'?'

Printed in Great Britain
by Amazon